TALES FROM A FINNISH TUPA

TALES *from* A FINNISH TUPA

By
JAMES CLOYD BOWMAN
and MARGERY BIANCO

From a Translation by
AILI KOLEHMAINEN

Pictured by
LAURA BANNON

University of Minnesota Press
Minneapolis • London

Published by the University of Minnesota Press
111 Third Avenue South, Suite 290
Minneapolis, MN 55401-2520
http://www.upress.umn.edu

Library of Congress Cataloging-in-Publication Data

Bowman, James Cloyd, 1880–1961.
Tales from a Finnish tupa / by James Cloyd Bowman and Margery Bianco ; from a translation by Aili Kolehmainen ; pictured by Laura Bannon. — 1st University of Minnesota Press ed.
p. cm.
Summary: An illustrated collection of folktales from Finland, including the magical tale "Vaino and the Swan Princess," the humorous story "The Pig-headed Wife," and the fable "The Bear Goes Fishing."
ISBN 978-0-8166-6768-0 (pb : alk. paper)
1. Tales—Finland. [1. Folklore—Finland.] I. Bianco, Margery Williams, 1881–1944.
II. Kolehmainen, Aili. III. Bannon, Laura, ill. IV. Title.
PZ8.1.B67Tal 2009
398.2'094897—dc22
2009013946

Printed in the United States of America on acid-free paper

The University of Minnesota is an equal-opportunity educator and employer.

16 15 14 13 12 11 10 09   10 9 8 7 6 5 4 3 2 1

CONTENTS

CONTENTS—Continued

I
TALES OF MAGIC

THE SHIP THAT SAILED BY LAND AND SEA

There were once three brothers. Onni, the eldest, traded in furs and made a great deal of money. Urho, the second brother, sold fine linens, and he too was very prosperous. But the youngest brother didn't do as well. He was only a chimney sweep, and as his face was always black with soot his family nicknamed him Noki.

The country where these three brothers lived was ruled by a king who was said to be very, very wise. He had an only daughter, Marja, whom he loved dearly. When Marja was old enough to marry, the King sent his heralds through the countryside with these tidings:

"Hark ye, hark ye! This is the King's proclamation! The King will give his daughter in marriage to the man who brings to his palace a ship that can sail both on land and sea."

[1]

This message set all the people wondering, and they could talk of nothing else. A ship that could sail by land and sea! After a while they decided that the King must love his daughter so much that he never wanted to part with her. For who ever heard of a ship like this!

But still in every part of the kingdom the young men all began building ships, each in the hope that he might find some magic way to make his own particular ship travel by land as well as by water.

Onni, the eldest of the three brothers, at once hired all the carpenters he could find and sent them into the deep wild forest to lay the keel for a large vessel. As Onni himself set out to direct the work, there at the edge of the forest he met an old woman lying by the roadside. She was so wasted and feeble that she could not stand alone, but she grabbed at Onni's boot as he went by, and called to him:

"Help me, brother, help me to my feet! Don't leave me here to die all alone!"

But selfish Onni was in such a hurry to get to his ship-building that he only shouted over his shoulder:

"I'm sorry, my poor woman, but I can't stop to help you. My carpenters have gone ahead and I must hurry to direct them."

A little further along the way Onni met a feeble old man hobbling along on a crutch.

"Please take me with you," the old man called. "I can be a very useful servant."

"O-ho," said Onni bitterly, "you must be crazy! You are old and worn-out and you need looking after your-self!"

And he pushed the old man aside and hurried on his way. When he came to the middle of the deep wild forest there were all his carpenters already hard at work felling trees. Soon they were laying the keel of a great vessel. For many days they labored and presently the masts of the ship towered high among the trees and the prow lifted its head in pride.

At last came the moment when Onni commanded his carpenters to set the great ship in motion. They pushed and they pulled and they tugged and they sweated, but the ship only sank deeper and deeper into the ground. And when at last they had tired themselves out they were so discouraged that Onni dismissed them, and they all went home.

When Onni returned his two brothers were very curious to know what had happened. They asked him how his ship had turned out.

"Yes," he told them, "I built a beautiful ship. It was strong enough to battle the storms and its masts outtopped the tallest fir trees. But we could not make it move on land. I had to leave my fine ship there to rot in the deep wild forest. . . . The King only makes fools of us all with his crazy ideas. Who ever heard of a ship that would sail by land and sea!"

But Urho, the second brother, was not a bit discouraged by Onni's failure. He too hired carpenters and sent them into the deep wild forest. And as he hurried after them, he too met the old woman by the roadside and the old man with his crutch. They each shouted after him, but Urho was too selfish and in too much of a hurry to pay any attention to them.

He shouted his orders and drove his men to work, and soon his ship too was finished, and very proud it looked. Then he commanded his workmen to set it moving. They too pushed and they pulled, and they tugged and

[3]

they sweated, but for all their pains the ship only planted itself deeper and deeper in the ground. And so Urho too in the end had to send his workmen home. When he came back and Onni and Noki asked about his ship he blamed the King, saying:

"The King knows very well that no seagoing vessel can travel by land! We are all fools to listen to him."

But Noki laughed at the failure of his older brothers, for he was young and strong and he still had his dreams.

"Who knows," he said to himself, "if I try, I may yet win the hand of the Princess."

Soon after, Noki set out all alone. He slung a wallet across his shoulder and took along a few meat bones for soup and three loaves of bread, for this was all he had money to buy. As he walked he sang a merry tune to keep up his courage. When he grew tired he repeated a little verse that his grandmother had taught him when he was a tiny child sitting on her knee.

> Nyt sitä mennään Nokin kanssa
> Iilamanssiin, Iilamanssiin . . .
> Now Noki goes to Iilamanssi,
> Iilamanssi, Iilamanssi,
> Poku poku poku, poku poku poku,
> Poku poku poku,
> Rompoti, rompoti, rompsus!

Before Noki had gone very far he came upon the old woman lying beside the road. She said:

"Help me, brother, help me! I am dying here all alone. I am so weak for want of food that I haven't the strength to move another step."

Noki was sorry for the old woman. He gathered a few sticks of brushwood, built a fire and made broth, and broke some bits of bread into it. When the old woman had eaten, he helped her to her feet.

[4]

The old woman thanked Noki with tears in her eyes. Then she took a curious copper whistle from a pocket in her skirt, gave it to him, and said:

"My good young man, you have surely a heart in your breast. Here is a whistle for you. Prize it as you prize your life, for you will find it of the greatest use if ever you are in need."

Noki thanked her and thrust the whistle in his pocket.

Soon after he entered the forest he met the old man leaning on his crutch.

"Where are you going?" asked the old man.

"I am going to build a ship," Noki said. "A strange ship it will be, too, for it will sail both on land and by sea. It's like this; when I have my ship all built I shall sail in it to the King's palace, for I mean to marry Marja, the King's beautiful daughter."

"Then take me along with you," said the old man. "I'll gladly be your servant, and you'll find me a useful one, too."

"You are too weak to travel far," Noki said as he began to open his knapsack. "First I'll make you some broth and we'll share this bread. Then, if you feel stronger, we'll see about it."

"All right," said the old man. "While you are making the broth, I'll be looking about the forest to see what timber we can find for your good ship."

Noki set to work. He found a spring of sparkling water, built a fire of twigs and began to cook the broth. When the broth had come to a boil, all at once he heard a great noise and a crashing. He looked up from his pot, and there was a tall stately ship moving towards him between the trees. And there at the rudder stood the old man, leaning on his crutch.

[5]

At this sight Noki knew that his new friend, the old man, was a great magician.

The old man stopped the ship beside Noki, climbed down and ate the broth and the bread which Noki had made ready for him. And when he had done eating, he said:

"Noki, you have been kind to me and I have helped you. Now let me whisper a charm in your ear:

Kulje, kulta laiva,
Kauas näeltä mailta
Mene Marjan luokse.
Go thou, golden ship,
Far from these low lands
To my Marja's side.

"Now climb into the ship, take good hold of the rudder, repeat this charm, and the ship will obey your will."

"But you must come with me," Noki said.

"I am too old. I should only be in your way. But you will meet others who will be glad to go with you."

Noki thanked the old man again, climbed aboard the ship, took the rudder in his hand and repeated the charm. And sure enough, the great ship began to move out towards the open fields and the sea.

After a time Noki saw a tall thin man who called to him:

"Where are you going?"

"To marry the King's daughter."

"Then take me with you, I am Lihan-Syöjä, the Meat-Eater. You will surely need me."

Noki laughed, for he had no meat left even for himself. But he repeated the charm, and stopped the vessel.

"All right, if you think you can be of any use to me, come along."

[6]

Again the ship set forth. Soon a short, stout man with a red jolly face called to them:

"Where are you going? I am Viinan-Juoja, the Wine-Drinker. Take me with you."

"All right. Come along!"

When the ship reached the seashore, a third, and then a fourth man called out:

"I am Kuuman-Jäähyttäjä, the Heat-Cooler. . . . I am Pitkän-Juoksija, the Far-Runner. . . . You will need us before you reach your journey's end."

"Very well," Noki laughed back. "Come along. The more the merrier!"

After a long stormy voyage across the open sea, Noki brought his ship to shore on the wide curving beach of white sand just before the King's palace.

Here he repeated the charm, and the great ship moved up the shore and across the King's garden. The soldiers shouted to it to stop, but the ship kept right on its way, never stopping till it reached the inner court yard door. Meanwhile the soldiers all rushed into the palace shouting.

"O King, a wondrous thing has happened! The ship that sails by land and sea is standing at your very door!"

When the King came out to look there was the ship, and there was Noki calling to him.

"O King, here is the ship you asked for. I have come in it to marry your beautiful daughter Marja. May we be married right away?"

"Not so fast, not so fast, young man," said the King. "There will be time enough after I have looked your ship well over."

"Your wish is law," smiled Noki as he stepped down beside him.

[7]

Now Marja was peeping through a crack in the window, and when she saw Noki's smiling face she was delighted, for he was a fine handsome lad with broad shoulders, and he carried his head like a prince.

The King peered at every part of the ship, hoping to find something wrong about it, but it was perfect through and through. At last he said: "Who are you, my young adventurer?"

"I am Noki, the Chimney Sweep."

"A chimney sweep!" shouted the King, out of all patience. "And you expect to marry the Princess? What nonsense!"

"But O King, I am rich," said Noki. "I have my happy heart and I have my dreams. Yes, and I have four faithful friends with me in my ship."

"If you think yourself so clever," said the King, "I will give you a bit of work to do. When you've finished that you can come back to me, and then maybe we'll talk about the Princess."

"O King, your wish is law," Noki smiled. "I will try any task you set me."

"All right. There are three hundred wild rabbits hopping about my fields and hedges. Herd them together here in the inner court yard of my castle before the sun goes down tonight."

Noki looked downcast, for this seemed an impossible task.

"Very well, O King, I will do my best to please you," he said, and set forth.

In and out Noki walked, round the hedges and across the field. He tore his clothes and he scratched his face and hands on the thorns, but not a rabbit did he see. They were far too clever for him. Here and there he

[8]

peered, and all the while the sun was slipping lower and lower down the western sky. At last Noki sank down under a fir tree, and racked his brains as to what to do.

By chance his hand went into his pocket, and there he felt the copper whistle. He drew it out and stared at it. And he thought that he heard a tiny whisper. "Noki, Noki, blow upon me!"

No sooner had Noki begun to blow than a strange thing happened. At every note from the whistle dozens of rabbits, large rabbits, small rabbits, white rabbits, grey rabbits, all sorts and kinds of rabbits that anyone could imagine—hopped out from their hiding places and came running toward him.

Noki was so happy that he sprang to his feet and ran as hard as he could towards the court yard. As he ran he blew on the whistle, and all those three hundred rabbits leaped after him as though bewitched.

When he reached the court yard with all the rabbits following after him, the King and the soldiers could hardly believe their eyes. Marja was still peeping through the window, and now she felt surer than ever that this strange young man was someone very wonderful indeed. She almost wished she was a rabbit herself, to come leaping at the sound of that magic whistle.

"*Now* may I marry Marja?" asked Noki.

"There's another job that needs doing," said the King. "First you must eat up all the meat in my castle before morning."

"May I ask one of my good friends to help me?" Noki asked.

"You may ask them all, if you like," said the King, for he knew that the castle was stocked with so much meat that it would take a whole army to eat it up.

[9]

So Noki called his friend Lihan-Syöjä, the Meat-Eater, and said to him: "Now I know why you asked to come with me. Did you hear what the King said?"

"You may count on me," said Lihan-Syöjä.

When morning came the King was astounded. He even had to go without his bacon for breakfast. High and low, there was not a scrap of meat left in the castle even big enough to make broth with.

"But there's another job to do, still," said the King, who was beginning now to feel uneasy. "Before the sun sets, you must drink every drop of wine in my cellars."

Noki smiled, and he called his friend Viinan-Juoja, the Wine-Drinker. Before nightfall the King was sorry for his words, for the last of his kegs and bottle and jugs was emptied, and he himself had to go to bed thirsty.

By this time he was getting quite out of patience.

"There is another task still before you may ask for the Princess," he said. "You and all your friends must go into my *sauna* and bathe."

This time, the King thought, he would surely settle them, for he had ordered his servants to heat the bathhouse stones so hot that anyone who entered it would be scalded to death.

But by this time Noki knew the King's tricks. So he sent his friend Kuuman-Jäähyttäjä, the Heat-Cooler, in first. At the Heat-Cooler's third breath, the bathhouse became comfortable. Noki and the rest of his friends walked in, enjoyed their bath, and returned to the King smiling.

"Now you'll have to give me your daughter," said Noki.

"Not so fast, young man," the King replied. "I like your courage, but there is one more job still before

[10]

you. Do this, and then I will gladly give you my dear daughter, the Princess Marja. Before sunrise tomorrow you must fetch me a brimming measure of the water of life which is hidden behind the seven seas."

Noki was silent, for this was surely the hardest task of all. But his friend Pitkän-Juoksija, the Far-Runner, said:

"I'll gladly fetch you a measure of the water of life from behind the seven seas!"

"Go then," said Noki, "and my blessing be upon you."

In a flash Pitkän-Juoksija disappeared, and Noki and his friends sat down in the ship to wait for his return. All night long they waited, torn between hope and fear. But when dawn began to streak the eastern sky with gold there stood the Far-Runner before them. In one hand he was carrying a large birch bark bowl filled with the water of life.

When the King saw this priceless treasure, he was so happy that he not only gave the Princess Marja to Noki, but half of his kingdom as well.

With such friends to help them, it isn't any wonder that Noki and Marja lived happily for many many years.

THE MEN OF THE WALLET

Once upon a time there was a poor peasant named Timo. Although he worked for a wealthy farmer, Timo himself had nothing at all. When *Joulu*, the Christmas feast, came round and everyone else was making merry, Timo felt very sad. He had no stuffed pig to set on the family table. So he went to his master, whose name was Julma, and said:

"Master, I have no Christmas dinner for my family. If you will lend me a small pig now, I will promise to give you back a large fat hog next summer."

Because it was the season of good will rather than because he felt sorry for Timo, his rich master lent him the pig, and Timo went home very cheerfully with his Christmas dinner.

Timo was a man of his word, and did not forget his promise. He raised a pig and brought it to Julma next fall. But Julma was in a very bad temper that day, and as soon as he set eyes on the pig that Timo had brought he began to curse him roundly.

"*Mene Hiiteen porsainesi* (To the devil with you and your piglet)!" he shouted. "Go to Hiisi with your miserable pig!"

Timo took his words seriously, and started off with the pig. After walking for two days, he met a stranger on the road who asked him:

"My good man, where are you going with that pig?"

"My lord and master, Julma, bid me take it to Hiisi," Timo answered. "But I don't know whether I'm on the right road. Can you tell me the way?"

"You're going in the right direction," said the stranger. "Just follow the white crosses along the road and you'll come to Hiisi before long."

Timo thanked him, and kept on his way. After trudging many miles, at last he saw the castle turrets of Hiisi rising in the distance. When he reached the doorway he saw the King's two daughters guarding the entrance. On one side of the doorway there hung a giant sword and on the other a huge bottle.

"O-ho," said Timo, "that's a mighty big sword! Tell me, are there any giants left nowadays strong enough to wield it?"

"That is our father's sword," the girls answered. "He has only to take two stout draughts from this bottle and the sword is as light as a feather in his hand."

"I wonder what would happen to me if I drank my fill from such a bottle," said Timo, joking. "It might even give me courage to face the King, your father."

"Take a drink by all means, and see!" the girls laughed back.

When Timo reached the entrance to the King's inner chamber he saw that the door was hung with human bones. He was met by a guard so enormous that Timo felt like a child before him.

"What are you doing here, my good man?" asked the guard in a deep gruff voice.

"Julma, my lord and master, told me to take this pig to Hiisi."

"Very well, you may enter," returned the guard, pleased with Timo's courage. "And if the King asks you what gift you want in return for your present, tell him: 'The mill of Hiisi.'"

When Timo was shown into the presence of the King, he fell on his knees and dared not look the King in the face. He said humbly:

"Julma, my lord and master, bade me bring you this pig, O King."

The King was touched by Timo's frankness and humility. He said:

"Return my thanks to Julma, your master. But you, my honest man, who had the patience to bring his present all this long way, what can I give you from my treasury?"

"I do not know, most gracious King," stammered Timo, who was beginning now to feel a little frightened by his own audacity.

"You may have anything that you want," the King added.

"Then I would like the Mill of Hiisi."

The Mill was brought and, bowing low, Timo left the King's presence. When he parted with the guard at the door he said:

[14]

Timo spread the magic tablecloth

"And now that I have the Mill, what use can I make of it?"

The guard smiled.

"This is a magic Mill," he said. "Whenever you are hungry and in need of bread just turn the handle, and you will get all the flour you want."

Timo thanked the guard for his good advice, tucked the Mill under his arm and started homeward.

When darkness overtook him he stopped at a poor *tupa* (a cottage) by the roadside and asked for a night's lodging.

"You may sleep here if you like," said the woman of the house, "but I have no food. There has been a drought in the land and we are all starving."

"Don't worry about the food," said Timo. "Just fill your pot with water and set it to boil. I'll provide the meal for the porridge."

The woman did as he told her and Timo set the Mill down and began to turn the handle. At once the meal began to pour out in a golden stream and overflow the table.

When the woman saw this magic Mill of Hiisi, she wanted it for her own, and could think of nothing but how to get hold of it.

After a hearty meal of porridge, Timo stretched himself out and fell sound asleep. In the middle of the night the woman stole the Mill from his bedside and set her own worthless hand mill there instead.

Timo woke early in the morning, ate a good breakfast of porridge and went his way cheerfully, never dreaming of the trick the woman had played on him. When he reached home he called to his wife.

"Helka, Helka, come quick! We'll never be poor

[16]

again. We'll have food for the rest of our lives. See what I've brought you from Hiisi!"

Helka came running. Timo had set the Mill on the table and was turning the handle with all his might. But turn as he would, no meal came out.

"What are you making all this fuss for about an old worn-out hand mill!" Helka cried, out of all patience with him. "Have you gone crazy? Fancy carting a useless thing like that all the way from Hiisi!"

Timo was ready to burst into tears. He said:

"Helka, the King has played a trick on me. I shall take this Mill back at once."

Again he trudged patiently all those long miles to Hiisi. When he met the guard at the King's door he said:

"I don't want this hand mill. It gave meal only the first time when I turned the handle. Now it won't work!"

The guard looked down his long nose at Timo and replied in a gruff voice:

"The King may be so angry that he'll order your head cut off when he knows you are back again. But if he should change his mind and offer you something else instead, ask for the Tablecloth and you'll never repent your bargain."

Again Timo bowed low before the King, and told his story.

"And what do you want in exchange?" asked the King angrily.

"The Tablecloth," Timo answered, almost shaking with fear.

"Take it, and get out of my sight!" the King growled.

Timo came out as white as a ghost. He asked the guard:

"What can I do with this?"

"Spread the cloth on the table, and it will be covered with all the food you want."

Timo thanked the guard and set out. As he hurried homeward he thought: "This time I will make Helka happy."

When night overtook him he found himself once more at the dishonest woman's *tupa*. The woman had seen him coming, and had taken care to hide the Mill so that he would not suspect her.

"My good woman," Timo said, "for the second time I must ask you for a night's lodging."

"Come in and welcome. I can give you a bed, but you must furnish your own food. The weather has been so dry that we are starving."

"Don't worry about food," said Timo, as he spread his magic cloth over the bare table.

And there was the table covered with every good thing one could wish! In the middle was a savory *Kala kukko*, or a baked fish inside a huge loaf of rye bread. There were great jugs of milk and a jug of sweet red wine.

Timo was tired from his long journey and as soon as he had eaten he stretched out and fell sound asleep.

"This magic cloth," said the dishonest woman to herself," is even better than the Mill. It is better than eating at the King's table!"

And while Timo slept she managed to exchange one of her old tablecloths for Timo's magic Tablecloth.

Early next morning Timo hurried home, thinking only of the joy he was bringing to Helka.

"Now we need never be hungry again," he cried as he strode into the house. "Just look, Helka, what I have brought you this time!"

And he spread his cloth on the clean table, trembling with excitement. But nothing happened. The Table-cloth was perfectly bare.

"Now I know you are crazy!" Helka scolded. "First you bring an old worn hand mill and now you come with a shabby old tablecloth that's only fit for rags! Was ever such a foolish man born!"

"I am sorry, Helka," Timo sighed. "Someone has certainly played me a trick again. But don't lose trust in me. I've still strength enough in my old bones to make one more journey to Hiisi."

And again he started out. But he was tired and stiff and heavy-hearted. By the time he came within sight of the castle turrets, he felt too weary to take another step. So he sat down to rest by the roadside for a long while before he could muster courage to venture once more into the King's presence.

"A second time I come to return the King's gift," he said humbly as he stood before the guard at the King's inner chamber. "For again the gift has proved worthless."

"You're here every day," returned the guard harshly as he looked down over his long cold nose. "I shouldn't be surprised if the King really has your head cut off this time. But if by any chance he does let you exchange your gift, be sure and ask for the Wallet."

This time Timo bowed lower than ever before the King, then lifted his honest face.

"What! You here again?" the King shouted.

"The cloth, O King, has turned out worthless," Timo humbly answered. "I do so want Helka, my wife, to know that I am not really crazy. I have tried so hard to make her happy."

[19]

"O-ho!" laughed the King boisterously. "I pity the wife indeed who has to live with a man as hard to please as you are! Choose the gift you want for this one time more, but if ever you bother me again I'll have your head cut off."

Timo got the Wallet, and when he came trembling from the King's inner chamber he asked the guard:

"What use can I make of this Wallet, now that I have it?"

"Use, you fool?" the guard shouted. "Why, this is the King's most valued possession! When you are in need of help, open the Wallet and say: 'Out, boys, out of the bag!' At once men will leap out of it to do your bidding. But let me give you one bit of advice. Never call the men from the Wallet unless you have work for them to do, or else they will turn upon you and beat you. Now begone! And if you prize your own head never tempt the King again as long as you live!"

Timo thanked the guard, and for the third time he started on his long, hard journey homeward. But now his heart was so full of hope that he forgot his weariness.

Nightfall found him once more at the *tupa* of the woman who had twice so neatly deceived him. Again she had seen him coming, and had hidden the Mill of Hiisi and the Magic Tablecloth.

"A third time I must ask shelter for the night," Timo said.

"You are welcome to a bed," the woman replied, "but unless you have brought food you must needs go hungry, for the famine still rages."

Timo took the wallet from under his arm and shouted:

"Out, boys, out! Bring me food for my dinner."

Two young men leaped from the Wallet at his words,

and set the table with food fit for a king. As soon as they had finished, Timo opened the wallet again and shouted: "Back, boys, back into the Wallet!"

They obeyed instantly. Timo closed the Wallet, sat down and ate his fill. Soon after dinner he fell once more into a deep sleep.

But this time, in the middle of the night, he was roused by cries and howls from the woman of the house, mingled with the sound of blows.

"Stop beating me, stop beating me and I'll give back the Magic Mill! I'll give back the Magic Tablecloth I stole from your master! Only stop beating me!"

Now Timo knew who it was that had played tricks on him and robbed him. It was not the King who was to blame, but the woman of the *tupa*. He rose hastily, called his men back into the wallet, snatched up Mill, Wallet and Cloth and started off through the night.

As he hurried along homeward in the darkness he kept saying over and over: "Now Helka will be happy! Now she'll know that I'm not crazy after all!"

Soon he had reached his own *tupa*. Day was just dawning.

"See, Helka, see! Look at the grand gifts I've brought you from Hiisi!"

Helka sniffed. She had heard enough about Hiisi and she wasn't going to be fooled again by this crazy husband of hers. But as she stood there, sniffing, Timo turned the Magic Mill, and before her astonished eyes out poured the golden meal. He spread the Magic Tablecloth, and there on their table lay good food of every kind. He opened the Wallet and shouted:

"Out, boys, out, and serve Helka as if she were the Queen!"

When she saw all these wonders Helka was near to weeping.

"At last, Timo," she said, "at last I do appreciate all the hard work you have done for me!"

After some weeks of feasting Timo called his men out of the Wallet and told them to build him a castle. They made him a mansion much finer than that of his master, Julma. All around it they planted a garden with beautiful trees and flowers, and in it set a pool that sparkled in the sunlight.

It was not long before Julma, the rich farmer, heard the gossip about Timo's house and came prowling around to see for himself what all the talk was about. But Timo happened to see him from a distance, and said to his men:

"Out, boys, out. Turn yourselves into an armed guard and let no man enter my palace."

The boys did as they were bid, and when Julma drew near he saw the gate so bristling with soldiers that he went back to his own home in fear. After this Timo began to feel a bit set up and proud of himself. He even wrote a letter to the king of his own country, asking him to come and dine.

The King however was himself a proud and haughty man. He asked:

"Who is this upstart peasant that dares to put on such airs? Send twenty of my best men, and tell them to thrash him till he comes to his right senses again."

Timo saw the soldiers in time, and ordered his men out of the Wallet. They fell upon the King's soldiers and beat them up soundly. When the King's men returned, rather shamefaced, to the royal palace they said:

"It is most extraordinary! A few weeks ago in that

spot there was only a miserable peasant's *tupa;* now there stands the most marvelous castle we have ever set eyes on. As soon as we drew near to it, men of supernatural power fell upon us and we were as babes in their hands. After they had beaten us they said:

'Take this message to your lord and master. Timo, the King's loyal subject, invites the King and Queen to dinner to celebrate the housewarming of his new castle.' "

When the King's messenger came to Timo's castle to arrange for the royal visit, he was received nobly. On his return he said:

"O King, something wonderful has certainly happened to this Timo. He has either a magician working for him, or some powerful charm. For both within and without his castle he has everything that the heart of man could desire."

Upon the King's arrival, the men of the Wallet escorted him into the castle with great ceremony. They placed the King at a table set with the most costly silver.

Then Timo said:

"O King, if you will name your favorite dishes, I will see that they are brought to you without delay!"

It was as Timo said. Whatever the King desired, it was brought to him instantly. Never had he been so royally served before, even in his own palace.

When he left he took Timo's hand kindly and said:

"You have won my highest respect. From now on I shall call you 'brother.' "

Before long a great war broke out. The King's army was routed in every battle. At last in despair the King remembered Timo, and sent a messenger to fetch him to the palace. Timo did not forget his Wallet.

[23]

"Let me try my luck against the King's enemies," he said.

"You don't mean single-handed?" cried the King in astonishment.

"I have powers at my command such as you have never seen," added Timo modestly.

"Yes, I have heard a goodly report of your magic soldiers," returned the King grimly. "Go then, and send me tidings of what happens."

Timo hastened to the battle front with his Wallet. The enemy looked amazed to see a single man coming towards them. But in a flash Timo opened his Magic Wallet and shouted:

"Out, boys, out every one of you! Fall upon the enemies of the King!"

Out hopped the men in battalions and companies and regiments—an endless host of them. They fell with such haste upon the enemy that the whole army took to its heels and ran like one man, leaving blood-stained tracks behind them.

The King was so pleased that he made Timo an honorary general upon the spot, with permission to own his land and his castle untaxed. And Timo and Helka spent many happy years together.

THE MOUSE BRIDE

Once there was a laborer named Pekka, who was always worried about the future. He was so anxious to know what might be going to happen that one day he went to an old Lapland woman, and asked her to tell him his fortune.

The old Laplander woman said:

"You will have three sons. As each son is born, you must plant a tree for him, and you must call that tree by the same name that you give your son. When the boys are grown to manhood and want to marry, tell each one to cut down his own name tree, and in whichever direction the tree falls, that way must he travel to find his wife. Mark my words well, and you will have good fortune."

Pekka did as the old Laplander woman told him. When his first son was born he planted a birch tree, and called it Onni, after the baby's own name. When his second child was born a year later he planted an oak tree, and he named both the boy and the tree Arne. When the third child was born, Pekka planted a fir tree, and named both the child and the tree Jukka.

As the boys grew, the trees grew, and by the time the three sons were grown men there stood their name trees, tall and fair with spreading branches.

One day Pekka's three sons came to him and said:

"Father, surely it is time now for each of us to seek a wife."

"It is time," said Pekka. "But before you set out, each one of you must fell his own name tree. And whichever way the tree points as it falls, that way must you set out to seek your wife."

It so happened that Onni's, the eldest son's tree, fell in the direction of a rich man's house. Arne's oak tree fell in the direction of a farmer's *tupa*. But when it came to Jukka, the youngest son's name tree, that fell in the direction of no house at all, but only by the deep forest.

Each son accepted his fate, and set forth in the direction his tree had pointed.

As Jukka walked on and on into the forest, he wondered what sort of bride he would find there. After walking for three days and seeing no one at all he came at last to a little clearing hidden among the trees, and there he saw a tiny *tupa* built of grey logs. He knocked at the door, but no one answered. Then he lifted the latch to look inside. The room was quite empty.

Jukka was tired after his long journey, and when he

found no one at home he was very disappointed. But there on the table in the middle of the room sat a little gray mouse with blue eyes and a queer white-tipped nose, looking at him.

"Welcome, stranger," said the little mouse. "Why are you so sad?"

"You would be sad, too," said Jukka, "if you had travelled three days and three nights, only to find that your bride was not at home."

"Then marry me," piped the little gray mouse.

"*Ka* (See)!" laughed Jukka bitterly. "Marry you, indeed! Why, you aren't even human."

"Marry me," said the little gray mouse again. "Marry me, and you will never be sorry for your bargain."

"*Ka,* I couldn't be worse off than I am now," said Jukka, "even if I did marry you."

"It's a bargain, then," said the mouse, and she began to dance about the table on her little gray feet. "When you come back, I'll be here waiting for you."

Jukka shut the door behind him and trudged sadly home again. When he reached the house his father and his two brothers asked him:

"What kind of wife did you find in the forest?"

"A very fine wife indeed," Jukka told them.

"Tell us all about her."

"There's nothing to tell, except that her eyes are very blue and her nose is very white."

"Blue eyes and a white nose! That's funny!" And they all began to laugh.

Then Onni and Arne began to tell their luck, bragging all evening about the wonderful brides they had found. But poor Jukka could only sit silent, and presently he went sadly to bed.

Next morning Pekka called his three sons to him, and said:

"Today you must each go and bring me back some piece of your bride's handiwork, so that I may judge which is the best. What do you say to a loaf of bread?"

"That's a good idea," agreed Onni and Arne, and they set out in haste. Poor Jukka trudged back to his mouse.

When he opened the door of the tiny gray *tupa,* there was his mouse bride sitting on the table.

"Do you seek something from me, *Kultani* (my dear one)," she asked, "or have you come to marry me?"

"My father has sent me to fetch a sample of your handiwork," Jukka answered. "Will you make me a loaf of bread?"

"All right," said the mouse bride. And she took a tiny reindeer bell in her paws and began ringing it. At the very first sound of the bell, in came a thousand mice all dancing on their toes. The mouse bride said to them:

"Each of you mice must bring me the finest grain of wheat you can find. Hurry up!"

Away scampered the thousand mice, and in no time at all there they were back again, each bringing a single grain of wheat. Then Jukka's bride took the grains of wheat, ground them up, and made a loaf of bread.

Jukka thought it very strange that a mouse could do all this, but he asked no questions. He merely thanked the mouse bride, took the loaf of bread under his arm and went home.

Onni had proudly brought a loaf of rye bread from his bride. Arne's loaf was of barley. But when their father saw that Jukka's loaf was baked from the finest wheat flour, he opened his eyes very wide. He examined each loaf in turn, then said:

"Now you must fetch me a piece of cloth woven by each of your brides. I wish to see which is the most skilful with her hands."

When Jukka opened the door of the tiny gray *tupa,* his mouse bride asked:

"Do you seek something from me, *Kultani,* or have you come to marry me?"

"My father has sent me," answered Jukka, "to fetch a piece of cloth that you have woven with your own hands."

"*Vai niin* (Is that so)!" cried the mouse bride. "That won't take long!"

Again she rang the tiny reindeer bell. Again the thousand mice came dancing in on their toes.

"Each of you mice must fetch me the finest shred of flax you can find," said the mouse bride. "And remember there's no time to waste!"

Away scampered the thousand mice, and in a moment back they all came again, each with his shred of the finest flax.

"Now you must all help me to weave it," said the mouse bride.

The mice all set to work busily. Some carded, others spun, the mouse bride herself wove, and in no time at all the piece of cloth was finished. Jukka was very surprised when his mouse bride folded up the cloth neatly, tucked it inside a nutshell and put the nutshell in his hand. He thanked her, thrust the nutshell in his pocket and hurried home.

His father and his two brothers were there waiting for him. Onni proudly showed his square of cloth, but it was hard and stiff. The cloth that Arne's bride had made was uneven and loosely woven. The father examined the two pieces, but said nothing. Then he turned to Jukka and asked:

"*Ka,* and where is your cloth?"

"There is so little of it, it is hardly worth the showing," Jukka said, taking the nutshell from his pocket.

When they saw the nutshell, Onni and Arne burst out laughing. But when their father opened it and drew out the cloth, so finely was the linen woven that there were fifty yards of it folded there! Pekka's eyes opened wide in wonder, for never had he seen anything to compare with this handiwork, but still he said nothing.

A few days after he again called his sons together.

"It is now the summer month," he told them, "and time for each of you to go and fetch his bride. I wish to see which of you has made the wisest choice. It is fitting that my sons be wed on Midsummer's Day!"

Onni and Arne fairly jumped for joy, and ran each to fetch his bride. But poor Jukka scarcely knew what to do. He set off slowly like a man who walks in a bad dream.

When he reached the tiny gray *tupa* he said to his mouse bride:

"Come now with me. My father wants to meet you."

"*Ka,* since it is his wish, let us go together," piped the mouse bride in her tiny treble voice.

She rang her reindeer bell, and this time there danced into the room five sleek gray mice harnessed to a carriage made of a chestnut burr with a toadstool for a canopy.

The mouse bride seated herself in the tiny carriage as stately as any queen, all ready to start.

"But how can I bring you to my father like this?" Jukka asked. "When my brothers see how small you are they will make fun of me, and my father will be angry."

"Don't be afraid," said the mouse bride. "If only you do as I tell you, dear Jukka, you'll be a happy man yet!"

The five sleek mice started off at a gallop, and Jukka walked slowly along beside the chestnut burr carriage. He did not know whether to laugh or cry.

On the second day of their journey they came to a bridge that crossed a river. The five gray mice started at a quick trot, with Jukka walking beside them. In the middle of the bridge they met a big peasant boy with a hard ugly face and broad shoulders. The boy growled:

"What do you think you're doing, walking beside this crazy mouse-carriage?"

And before Jukka could stop him, the peasant boy had given a kick with his clumsy foot. Pell-mell, the five gray mice and the tiny chestnut burr carriage and the little mouse bride all flew out into the running water. There was a splash, and they were gone.

Jukka was ready to fight, but when he looked round the boy had disappeared. So he turned to peer again into the running water. And then he saw five sleek gray horses drawing a glittering carriage out of the stream and up the bank. In the carriage, holding the reins, sat a lovely maiden. She drove the carriage up to the bridge and stopped beside Jukka, who stood tongue-tied with surprise.

"Aren't you coming with me the rest of the way?" she asked. But Jukka could only look stupid and rub his eyes.

"Don't you know me?" the maiden went on. "I am the mouse bride whom you agreed to marry. Get up here and ride beside me, and on the way I'll tell you how it all happened."

Jukka climbed into the carriage beside her. He took the reins into his own hands and as they drove along his bride told her story.

"I was once a king's daughter," she said. "But a Lapland witch-woman became envious of my beauty, and when I was fifteen she changed me and all of my servants into mice. The spell could not be broken until one young man should ask to marry me, and another should try to kill me by casting me into water. You, Jukka, became betrothed to me, and the peasant lad we just met on the bridge kicked me into the water to drown. So now the spell has been broken and here I am, my own self once more!"

When he heard this, Jukka was the happiest man in the whole world.

"And what shall I say," he asked, "when my father wants to know your name?"

"Call me Olga," said his bride.

"And now, Olga my sweetheart," Jukka said, "we must waste no time in getting home to keep our wedding feast. The village folk will all be there and we'll dance all day and all night."

As usual, Onni and Arne had returned first, and were there waiting with their father, but this time they had their brides with them. When they saw Jukka driving up in that grand carriage with his five fine horses, they couldn't believe their eyes. But the sight of Olga surprised them still more, for she was the most beautiful woman they had ever seen. As for their father, he couldn't keep his eyes off her, which made both Onni and Arne very jealous.

So the three sons were married in their father's house, which was all decked with green boughs and flowers.

The village musician came and played on his *kantele* (a Finnish harp) and sang while all the young folk of the village danced by moonlight. And old Pekka nodded his head in happiness to see his sons and daughters so gay.

When the last tune had been played and the last dance was over and the last toast drunk, Jukka and Olga climbed into their carriage and the five gray horses bore them swiftly back to the valley hidden away between the trees.

And there was a new surprise for Jukka, for the tiny gray *tupa* had turned into a King's castle.

"This is just as it all was when I was a child," smiled Olga, "before the Laplander woman worked her witchcraft on me."

And there it was, far from the busy world, that Jukka and his mouse bride lived happily ever after.

VAINO AND THE SWAN PRINCESS

Once upon a time there was a young man named
Vaino. He lived all alone in the deep forest, in a *tupa*
beside a small lake. One morning as he sat resting under
a tree, all at once he heard a beating of wings, and nine
snow-white swans swooped down from the sky and settled
upon the water near the shore. But when they caught
sight of Vaino, away they all flew again.

Vaino was so excited that the next morning he hid behind a stump to see if they would return. Sure enough
they did, and this time a strange thing happened. The
nine swans laid down their feathery robes on the shore,
and Vaino saw that they were nine beautiful maidens
who had come to bathe in the lake.

They were all beautiful, but one was more beautiful than the rest, with long golden hair and blue eyes. Vaino knew that she must be under the evil spell of some witch, and as he had fallen in love with her at first sight he wanted very much to free her.

As soon as the nine maidens left the water, they put on their feathery robes again and at once they became nine white swans that flapped their wings and flew off into the sky. Vaino hurried to the hut of an old Lapland woman who lived on the edge of the forest.

"How can I break the spell and free this beautiful maiden?" he asked her.

The old woman sat on her bench, her chin in her hand, rocking her body slowly back and forth. After mumbling to herself for a long time she said:

"Tomorrow, while the maiden is in the water, steal her feathery robe and burn it. Then the spell will be broken."

"But how can I win her love?" Vaino wanted to know.

"When the maiden calls to you the first time, you must answer with this charm:

Pala tuli, pala mieli,
Kaunis neitosen.

Burn, O fire, burn, O heart
Of maiden beautiful!

and at once her heart will burn with love for you."

Vaino thanked the old woman, and next morning he again hid himself behind the stump and waited. Before long he once more heard the beating of wings, and saw the glitter of white pinions against the sun. Once more the nine swan maidens swooped down, cast off their robes and began swimming in the water. Vaino, watching his chance, snatched up the robe belonging to the maiden he loved, and burned it. When the maidens smelled the burning and saw the smoke that filled the air, they were seized with terror; they rushed to their robes and eight of them flew off into the sky as swans.

But the ninth maiden ran about on the sands weeping.

"Who has stolen my robe!" she wailed. And in her despair she began to repeat a charm:

"If you are older than I, you shall be my father. If you are younger, you shall be my brother. If you are as old, and no older, you shall be my husband."

Vaino heard her voice, soft and pitiful, and answered her:

> Pala tuli, pala mieli
> Kaunis neitosen.

> Burn, O fire, burn, O heart
> Of maiden beautiful.

As he finished singing, he stepped from his hiding place, and when the maiden saw how strong and handsome he was she gladly gave him her hand.

"How glad I am," she cried, "that that witch's evil spell is broken!"

"But how came you to be changed into a swan?" Vaino asked.

The maiden told him that the witch had hated her father, who was a king, and had wreaked her spite on his nine daughters.

"Come with me now to my father's castle," she said to Vaino," for you shall be my husband from now on."

The King was delighted to see his daughter back again

[36]

in her true form, but when it came to Vaino he was not so well pleased, for Vaino was of lowly birth. He thought a while, and said:

"First you must go into the heavens and fetch me the golden chains that hang from the clouds. Then we will talk about marrying my daughter."

Vaino set out on his journey with a heavy heart. He had never even heard of the golden chains that hang from the clouds, and had not the least idea how to set about finding them. But after he had walked a long way, thinking and thinking about it, he remembered the old Lapland woman who lived on the edge of the forest, and he hurried to her hut.

"How can I find the golden chains that hang from the clouds?" he asked her.

Again the old Lapland woman sat with her chin in her hands and rocked slowly back and forth for a long time, saying at last:

"Take the horse I shall give you. Close your eyes, and ride over mountain and valley, through river and forest. Ride without stopping until you feel your horse slipping from beneath you. Keep your eyes tight shut but stretch your two hands upward. Clutch at the air as the horse slips away, and you will feel the golden chains in your hands."

Vaino did as the old woman bade him. He rode over mountain and plain, over land and sea. All the time he kept his eyes tightly closed, though he was very curious to know where his horse was carrying him. At last he felt the horse slip from beneath him; he reached his arms upward and clutched at the air. And suddenly the heavy golden chains were in his hands.

In the same breath he felt himself falling—down, down

and ever down—through the empty air. He held his breath and clutched the gold chains tightly. When he opened his eyes again, he was in a strange country. Everywhere about him stretched a barren plain, with only a few dead stunted trees and here and there a withered flower. For this was the land of death.

In confusion Vaino walked this way and that, staring hopelessly about him. Presently he heard a clatter, and saw two skeletons fighting with drawn swords. Shivering with fear, Vaino drew near and asked them:

"Brothers, why are you fighting?"

"*Ka!*" shrieked one of the skeletons. "Here is a man at last who can settle our quarrel! It is like this. My neighbor here wants me to pay a debt which I have already paid to him, but he will not believe me."

"That's a queer thing," said Vaino. "But since you are both dead, there can be no question of debt between you. For surely the dead have nothing left to divide!"

"*Ka,* are we both dead?" cried the second skeleton.

"You speak truth," shrieked the first skeleton. "We will fight no more. Let us agree."

"And to you, O wise one," they said to Vaino, "here is a reward."

Then one of the skeletons thrust a cold gray stone into Vaino's hand, saying:

"Carry this stone with you, for you will find use for it before you again set foot in the land of the living."

And twining their bony arms about each other's necks, the two skeletons disappeared.

Vaino went his way, but soon he came upon two more skeletons, fighting just like the first. This time the quarrel was because one claimed the land belonging to the other. When they saw Vaino they asked him:

"Can you settle our quarrel for us?"

"How stupid you are to fight," said Vaino. "For since you are both of you dead, you can't have any land to fight about!"

This surprised them both, but they agreed that Vaino was right. So they made up their quarrel, giving Vaino another cold gray stone.

Presently Vaino came upon yet another pair of dead men, fighting because they could not agree whose wife was the cleverer and more beautiful. Again Vaino settled their quarrel, and for reward they, too, gave him a cold gray stone.

"I have enough of these cold gray stones," said Vaino to himself. "I must escape from this dreadful place, full of dead men fighting. But how?"

It happened that, as he spoke, he rattled the heavy golden chains he was still holding. And at the sound, at once there appeared before him every kind of sea creature, from a barnacle to a whale.

"What brings you here?" Vaino asked.

"You called us," said the sea creatures. "Do you not need us?"

"*Ka*, I need you indeed," Vaino said. "Carry me back from this pit of death to the land of the living."

"We are sorry," said the sea creatures, "but we cannot help you."

"Then go your ways!" cried Vaino, and he rattled the chains again.

This time there came running every kind of animal that dwells in the forest. From the rabbit and the squirrel to the wolf and the moose, they all gathered before him.

"Why do you gather?" Vaino asked them.

"You called us."

"What can you do?"

"Whatever you ask."

"Then carry me back to the land of the living," said Vaino.

"That we cannot do."

"Then you may go your ways," Vaino said, and they all disappeared.

A third time he rattled the heavy golden chains, and this time all the birds of the air fluttered down beside him.

"Why did you call us?" they asked.

"Carry me back to the land of the living," Vaino begged.

The birds looked at one another. Not one of them had the courage for such a flight. But at last a bald eagle flapped his great wings, and stepped forward.

"Have you the gold chains tight in your hands?" he asked.

"You can see for yourself," said Vaino.

"And have you the three cold gray stones?"

"I have them, too."

"Then climb on my back," said the bald eagle. "Put the golden chains in my beak for reins. Clutch the three stones tight in your hand and we will be off."

Vaino did as he was bid, and the eagle flapped his great wings and soared into the sky, cutting the winds and scraping the clouds. For a long time they flew, until the eagle grew tired. They were over the wide ocean now. The eagle said to Vaino:

"Drop your first cold gray stone into the water."

Vaino dropped the stone, and where it struck the water, there grew a huge mountain. The eagle settled down upon the mountain top and there they rested for the night.

In the morning the eagle took Vaino on his back again and they set forth, flying high above the clouds toward the land of the living. They were still above the wide ocean when the eagle again grew weary.

"Drop your second cold gray stone into the water," he said.

Vaino dropped his second stone. Again a tall mountain rose where the stone fell, and again they rested the night.

On the third day the eagle once more grew weary, and Vaino dropped his last cold gray stone into the sea. And once more they rested on the tall mountain that grew from the waters.

On the fourth day the eagle brought Vaino to the garden by the King's castle, setting him safely down among the flowers. Then he flapped his wings and flew off.

And there was Vaino's princess waiting for him, her golden hair shining in the sun and her eyes bluer than the blue sky.

"Whatever the King my father says, never will I let you go again!" she cried as she caught Vaino by the hand.

"Don't be afraid," said Vaino. "I have had my fill of long lonely journeys."

Together the lovers laid the golden chains at the King's feet, and the King was overjoyed.

"At last!" he cried. "With this golden chain I can break the spell that binds my eight other daughters!"

Then he gave Vaino and the Princess his blessing, and they all lived happily ever after.

HIDDEN LAIVA OR THE GOLDEN SHIP

In olden days there lived a woodsman whose name was Toivo. Every day, with his bow and arrows slung across his shoulder, he used to wander through the wild forests of Finland. One day in his wanderings he came to a high jagged mountain where no man had ever set foot before. For this was the mountain where the Gnomes lived, and there in a dark hidden cavern lay Hiitola, the Gnomes' home.

When the Gnomes saw Toivo, they all crowded round him and began shouting: "You come at just the right moment! If you will settle our quarrel and help us to divide our gold fairly between us, we will give you money and a golden ship."

It happened that the parents of these Gnomes had died just a few days before, and the Gnomes had fallen heir to all their wealth. They were very busy trying to divide it up. The whole mountain side was strewn with golden spoons and golden dishes and golden carriages. There was a lot of money, too, great shining gold pieces lying all about. The Gnomes were very greedy; each wanted to have more than his own share and so they couldn't come to any agreement about it all.

Toivo stared about him at all this wealth strewn around. More beautiful than the dishes or carriages was a ship of gold that stood on a high rock shining in the sun. The ship caught Toivo's eye at once.

"How do you make this ship go?" he asked the Gnomes.

The largest of the Gnomes stepped forward. He had a turned-up nose, a shaggy pointed red beard and short bandy legs. He hopped into the golden ship and said:

"Why, you just lift this upper what-you-may-call-it with your hand, and push the lower one with your foot, and the ship will race with the wind like a wild tern."

As soon as Toivo had learned the trick, he made a bargain with the Gnomes.

"If you will give me the golden ship and fill it with golden spoons and dishes, and fill my pockets with money, I'll show you how to settle your quarrel."

"Agreed!" shouted the Gnomes, and they began scrambling about in a great hurry to do as he asked.

Toivo set an arrow to his bow and said:

"I am going to shoot an arrow, and the first one to find it will be your King. He will settle your affairs."

"That's wonderful! Now we'll be happy again," shouted the Gnomes.

[43]

Toivo stretched his bow and sent the arrow whistling through the air. All the Gnomes went rushing after it. Then Toivo jumped into the golden ship, he pulled with his hand and he pushed with his foot, there was a loud whir-rr, and the ship leaped down the steep mountain and far out across the sea.

Soon after Toivo brought it to a perfect landing before the King's castle.

It happened that the King's daughter was on the castle steps at that very moment. She was sitting with her chin in her hands, dreaming of the day that some brave prince would come riding up to marry her, when all at once she saw the golden ship.

"This must surely be a prince from some wonderful country," she said to herself, "to come riding over land and sea in a ship like that!"

And she came dancing down the castle steps.

"Take me in your golden ship, dear Prince," she said, "and I will be your bride!"

But Toivo could only stammer, "Sweet Princess, you're making a big mistake, I'm merely Toivo, a common woodsman. I'm not good enough to touch the shoes on your feet. There are plenty of King's sons who would be glad and proud to be your husband!"

But the Princess was so excited about the golden ship and the golden spoons and the golden dishes that she didn't care whether Toivo was only a woodsman or what he was.

"It doesn't matter a bit," she said. "Take me in your ship, that's all, and I'll be your bride."

"You're making fun of me," Toivo answered her. "No one but a King's son would be good enough for the likes of you."

The Princess ran into the castle and back again, her arms heaped with costly clothes.

"Dress up in these," she laughed, "and you'll be a Prince too!" And back she ran to fetch food and drink.

Toivo was so humble he dared not even lay a finger on those fine clothes. He felt that he was not even good enough to be the Princess's servant. And he gazed at her in fear and trembling as she paced back and forth before the golden ship, begging him to marry her.

But at the end of seven days he saw that she was really unhappy because he refused her, so he said:

"Gentle Princess, if you really want to make a bargain with a humble woodsman, step into the ship."

As soon as she was seated, he fell on his knees and asked:

"Where would you like to sail, gentle Princess, in this golden ship?"

"To the very middle of the sea. I've heard tell there is an island there ten miles long where the berry bushes are loaded to the ground with red and purple fruit, and where the birds sing day and night."

Toivo pushed with his hand and pulled with his foot, and off flew the golden ship over land and sea. Soon it dived from the sky, right down to the center of an island, and stopped there. Toivo jumped out and ran to look for the purple and red berries.

The first berries that he found were yellow. Toivo tasted them, and before he knew what was happening he fell to the ground in a deep sleep. The Princess waited impatiently for him to come back. At first she thought he was lost. But after three days she decided that he had deserted her, and she grew very angry.

"Die here, you low-bred knave!" she cried. "I shall

turn the golden ship round and sail right home again."

So she pulled with her hand and pushed with her foot, and flew back to the castle, while poor Toivo still lay sprawled out on the ground fast asleep.

At the end of another day, Toivo woke up. He searched everywhere, but he could not find the golden ship nor the Princess. His beautiful golden spoons and dishes were gone, too. All he had left was a pocketful of money.

As he hunted high and low, he grew faint with hunger. Before him was a bush laden with purple berries. Toivo filled his left pocket with the fruit, thrust a berry into his mouth and began crunching it between his teeth. All at once he felt horns growing out from his head, monstrous pronged horns like the antlers of a wild moose. They were heavy and they hurt terribly.

"It would be better if I'd stayed hungry," he thought. "These horns are driving me crazy! If a ship should come, the sailors will take me for a wild beast and shoot me."

As he looked for some safe place in which to hide, he saw a bush with red berries on it. He filled his right pocket this time, and crunched one of the red berries between his teeth. No sooner had he done so than the heavy horns fell by magic from his head and he became the most handsome man in the world.

Next day a ship appeared over the edge of the sea. Toivo ran up and down the beach shouting to the sailors. "Take me with you, good friends, take me away before I die on this island. Bring me to the King's castle and I will pay you well."

The sailors gladly took Toivo and set him down before the King's castle. There he walked through the garden

She begged him to marry her

and came to a clear sparkling pool. He sat down on the edge of the pool and dipped his tired feet in the water.

It so happened that the King's Butler was coming to draw water. He said to Toivo:

"My good man, tired you may be, but if the King hears that you've been dipping your dusty feet into his drinking water, he'll have your head cut off!"

"My good sir," said Toivo, "the water will soon be clear again, but I'm sorry for my mistake. Let me show you a secret."

And he took a shining red berry from his right pocket and gave it to the Butler. The Butler crunched the berry between his teeth, and at once became the handsomest man in the kingdom, next of course to Toivo himself. He was so delighted that he hid Toivo in a corner of the pantry where the King would not find him.

At dinner time the Princess saw how wonderfully changed the Butler was in his looks, and it made her very curious.

"What has made you so handsome all of a sudden?" she asked him.

"I met a man in the garden who gave me a shining red berry," he whispered. "I ate it, and the charm worked. I became as you now see me."

"Find that man," the Princess said. "Tell him if he'll only make me beautiful too, I'll marry him."

"I'm afraid he's gone," the Butler said. "He wanted to hide, because he was afraid someone would cut his head off if they found him here."

"Tell him not to be frightened," the Princess said. "I will protect him. Bring him into the secret chamber and I'll give him food and drink."

The Butler went to fetch Toivo, and when they returned they found the Princess waiting with food and drink all set out. When the Princess saw Toivo, he was so handsome that she did not know him at all. While he was eating she said:

"If you can make me as beautiful as you are handsome, I'll be your bride."

Toivo became hot with anger, for he thought the Princess had grown tired of him on the island and had run away, stealing his golden ship and leaving him there to die. He did not know of the long time she had waited there.

"No, gentle Princess," he said, "I'm only a poor servant. There is many a king's son who would gladly marry you."

"Only believe me," she said. "I will dress you in a uniform of a General in the King's Army. I will fill your pockets with gold. I will give you a magic golden ship! Only please, please make me as beautiful as you are handsome, and let us be married."

"Very well," said Toivo at last. "Have it your way. Eat this berry."

He took a purple berry from his left pocket, and as the Princess crunched the berry between her teeth a pair of monstrous pronged horns grew out from her head, as heavy and huge as the horns of a wild elk!

As for Toivo, he got very frightened at what he had done, and ran off to hide.

The Princess set up a great hullabaloo, and everyone came running. When the King saw the horns he tried to cut them away, but they were hard as iron and firmly fixed to her head. So then he ordered his two strongest soldiers to follow behind the Princess everywhere she went and carry the weight of the horns while she walked.

No wonder the whole court was upset! The King and the Queen and all the ladies and gentlemen in waiting could talk of nothing but the poor Princess and her terrible plight. In despair the King at last sent soldiers into every part of his kingdom with this message:

"Whoever will cure the King's daughter by removing her monstrous horns shall receive the hand of the King's daughter in marriage and be raised to the highest command in the King's Army."

From every part of the kingdom came doctors and healers and magicians. They tried all their medicines and potions, all their spells and wonders. But it was wasted work, for the horns still remained.

At last, after many days, Toivo came forward from the crowd and knelt before the King, saying:

"O King, please let me try my cure."

"I doubt if you can do anything, my lad," the King said. "You can see for yourself how all these wise men have failed, one after another. They have eaten and drunk to their own luck, but my poor daughter remains the same."

"But, King, I am the only one who knows the right charm," Toivo begged. "If you'll let me try, I'm sure I can take away the horns."

"Try, then, and if the horns do fall from my daughter's head, I'll make you the highest general in my army."

"Send all these doctors and healers away," said Toivo, "and command your soldiers to make merry, for I will surely make your daughter the most beautiful woman in the kingdom!"

So the King commanded all the doctors and healers and magicians to go home, and the soldiers to make merry, while Toivo was left alone to work his cure.

Toivo said to the maidservant:

"Go, girl, and put dry sticks in the *sauna* (bath house) hearth. Make a hot fire to heat the stones in the Princess's bath house."

And to the page boy he said:

"Run quick to the deep wild forest, boy, and fetch me three long straight willow twigs. With these I will make the horns disappear."

The *sauna* was made ready with warm water and heated stones. The long straight willow twigs were brought and laid in the bath house, too. Then Toivo called for the Princess. He sent the maidservant outside and shut the door. He set the Princess on a bench. He tore the clothing from her shoulders and began to beat her soundly with the willow twigs.

"I'll teach you to run away with my golden ship and leave me to die in the middle of the sea!" he shouted between the strokes. "I'll teach you, you cruel woman, to steal my golden spoons and my golden dishes! I am Toivo, the man you promised to marry if I would take you to a far-off island! I'll teach you!"

The Princess's shoulders were soon red and welted from the blows of the willow twigs. She cried:

"Stop beating me, stop beating me, poor man, and I'll explain everything. Only stop, and I promise never to harm you again!"

"Very well then, explain," said Toivo gruffly.

"It was like this," the Princess began. "For three long days and nights I waited for you. I can't tell you how lonely it seemed, there on that island in the middle of the sea. Every moment I expected some horrible monster to come and swallow me alive. I felt sure you had deserted me, and you can't blame me for being so frightened that I flew back home in your golden ship. How can you doubt that I loved you from the very beginning, and still do!"

When Toivo heard this he threw away the willow twigs and fell on his knees before her. "Forgive me, forgive me for being angry with you, gentle princess! I will never lift my hand against you again."

As he spoke, Toivo drew a shining red berry from his right pocket. The Princess crunched it between her teeth; at once the ugly horns fell from her head and her face became as fair as a new-blown rose.

Toivo called the maidservant. She dressed the Princess in fine linen; upon her head she set the tall bridal crown, covered with jewels, and upon her feet soft shoes woven of the finest white birch bark in all the King's land.

When the people saw the Princess in her white robe, her thick golden braids falling to her knees, her blue eyes shining and her skin like the fairest rose-petal, they knew she had become the most beautiful woman in the kingdom.

The King was so happy he declared a holiday throughout the whole land. Everywhere people ate, drank and danced all night long.

Toivo became the King's highest general. He married his Princess and they all lived happily ever after.

ANTTI AND THE WIZARD'S PROPHECY

Many years ago it happened that two wizards were journeying through Finland. One evening they came to the *tupa* of a small farmer and asked if they might spend the night. As luck would have it the farmer's wife had that very evening given birth to a baby. So as the household was all upset and there was no room for strangers, the farmer asked the two wizards if they would mind sleeping in the *sauna*. They were both very tired so they readily agreed.

The farmer was so excited about the new baby he quite forgot to tell the wizards that he had already given the upper berth in the *sauna* to a travelling merchant who had also asked for a night's lodging earlier in the evening. The wizards saw the merchant lying there, but thought he was asleep, so they made up their own bed on the lower berth just beneath him, talking in whispers while they undressed.

"The farmer's wife has a new-born son," said the first
wizard. "Let us repeat a charm so that she may rest
easy during the night."
And together they repeated:

> "Mene kipu kauas täältä
> Lenna mustilla siivilla."
> Go forth, O pain!
> Fly on black wings
> Over Tuonela's dark river
> To Mountain of Misery, Kipuvuori.

"What kind of man do you think the child will be
when he grows up?" asked the second wizard.

The first wizard repeated another charm which helped
him to look into the future, and said:

"It is written that the boy will become the heir of
Ahnas, the wealthy merchant who is now sleeping on the
upper berth just over our heads."

But it happened that the merchant was not asleep,
and he heard everything the wizards said. Their prophecy worried him so much that he lay awake all night
planning how to rid himself of the child. When morning came, he again pretended to be asleep until he was
quite sure that the two wizards had started on their way.
Then he got up and went to speak to the farmer.

"You are poor," he said, "and have already many children to feed and clothe. I am rich. If you will give me
your new-born son, I will pay you a hundred roubles.
I will make him my heir, and he will be a comfort to me
in my old age."

The poor farmer was quite dazzled by this offer, for a
hundred roubles seemed to him a great deal of money.
He thought, too, that it would be a very good thing for
his son, so he sold the child to Ahnas then and there.

[54]

The farmer's wife sewed the baby into a warm leather bag so that only its tiny pink face showed, and with tears in her eyes put it into the merchant's arms. Ahnas laid the child on a bed of pine boughs in the bottom of his sleigh and set off for home.

But as soon as he was well out of sight of the house, he turned his horse and drove into the deep wild forest. There he left the child in the crotch of a gnarled pine tree and as he whipped his horse and drove hastily away he said to himself:

"Now I'm rid of you for good! You won't threaten my fortune any more."

But he was scarcely out of sight before a hunter happened to pass that way, and heard the baby crying. He took it down tenderly, carrying it in his arms to his *tupa* in the village. There he told the neighbors what had happened and they named the child Antti Puuhaara, which means "tree crotch."

Antti proved a strong healthy child, and as the years passed he grew into a strong and handsome young man.

It so happened that Ahnas, the merchant, stopped one day at the hunter's *tupa* to buy furs, and the hunter invited him to spend the night. During the evening the family gathered round the open hearth. They played the *kantele* and sang old-time songs and ballads. Ahnas became interested in the handsome youth whose voice was so clear and whose smile was so honest.

"What is your son's name?" he asked.

"Antti Puuhaara," the hunter told him. "It is a strange story. Many years ago, when he was a tiny baby, I found him sewed into a leather bag and hanging from the fork of a tree in the deep wild forest. I brought him home and he has become the joy and life of our household."

[55]

The merchant turned pale and his hands began to tremble, for again the fear of the wizard's prophecy was upon him. He disguised his feelings, but all that night he lay awake planning how he might make an end of Antti. In the morning he said to the hunter:

"I have to send an important message home. I am too busy buying furs to go myself, but if you will let Antti carry it for me I will pay you well for the trouble."

"*Ka*, indeed," said the hunter. "Antti will be only too glad to help you."

So Ahnas gave Antti a sealed letter to carry, and the youth started off gayly on his errand, never dreaming what the letter contained. Ahnas had written:

> Dear Wife,
>   Command my servants to hang by the neck the messenger Antti who brings you this letter. Fasten the rope to the limb of the birch tree that grows behind the garden wall.

Antti went whistling on his way. It was a long journey, and by the time he reached the foot of the mountains he was tired, so he lay down to rest. While he was sleeping two rogues happened along. They saw the letter, and thinking that it might contain money they opened it.

These two rogues knew Ahnas very well, for he had often cheated them in buying their furs. Here was a chance to pay him back. They guessed that he was playing a trick on the innocent Antti, so they changed the letter to read:

> Dear Wife,
>   Give the messenger Antti, who brings this letter, our daughter Alli for his wife without delay. Tell my servants to hang Musti, my dog, by the neck to the birch tree that grows behind the garden wall.

[56]

Then they made off, leaving Antti still sleeping. Presently Antti woke, not knowing that anything had happened, and continued his journey to the merchant's house. When he arrived the merchant's wife read the letter. She obediently gave her daughter to Antti in marriage and poor Musti, the dog, was duly hanged.

Many weeks later, when Ahnas returned home, he saw from a distance something black dangling from the birch tree.

"*Ka*," he said to himself. "Now I'm through with you. *You* will never be my heir!"

But when he drew nearer he had a great shock, for it was not Antti hanging from the tree branch, but Musti, his favorite hound. Worse still, when he entered the house there was Antti, his son-in-law, already taking his place in command of the household. Every one was very pleased and happy about it too.

Ahnas was a clever man, so he pretended that everything was just as he had expected. When he was alone with his wife he asked to see the letter, and all that night he lay awake planning how he might rid himself of Antti.

The next morning he greeted Antti very pleasantly, and said:

"Now that you're my son-in-law and heir to my estate, you must prove to me that you are really worthy of the honor. All my life long I have wondered what trade brings a man the greatest happiness. I'm tired of travelling here and there about the country buying furs, and I would like to change to some pleasanter business, if I only knew what. The only person in the world who can answer my question is Louhi, Mistress of the Northland. I myself am too old to make the long journey to her kingdom, so you must go for me."

Antti was quite willing to go. He was sorry to leave Alli, his happy bride, but he felt it a duty to do any service he could for this kind father-in-law. So he took a spear in his hand and set off with a brave heart.

After many days he came to Hiisi, the mountain where the gnomes dwell. At the very top of this mountain stood a tall giant, who carried clouds on his head and in his cap held imprisoned the eight winds of heaven. The giant saw Antti coming, and called to him:

"Where are you going, my lad?"

"I am bound for the far Northland, to ask Louhi what trade will bring a man most happiness."

"I have a question I'd like to have answered, too," the giant shouted. "My orchard used to bear fine fruit, but now the fruit molds before it is ripe. If you will ask Louhi what I can do about it, I will lend you my stallion to ride so you can travel faster."

"Surely I'll ask Louhi your question," said Antti, and he leapt on the stallion's back and galloped on.

As he rode, he heard ahead of him a great rumbling like thunder, and felt the earth tremble. Antti wondered what it could be. Presently he came to a stone castle. Outside the door stood a giant with an enormous key; he was trying to open the door, but the key would not turn in the lock. After trying a little while, he would lose patience and begin pounding on the door with his huge fists, so that the ground shook for miles around.

Antti was so frightened that it was all he could do to keep on his horse's back, but he managed to say:

"Good day and good luck to you!"

The giant turned round, scratched his ear angrily and returned:

"Where are you going, my lad?"

[58]

"I'm on my way to ask a question of Louhi, Mistress of the far Northland."

"*Ka*, then you can ask Louhi a question for me, too. I have lost the keys to my castle. If she can tell you where I can find them again, I'll make you a present of my own best handiwork."

"Surely I'll ask her that," said Antti, and he rode on with the speed of the wind.

Soon he came to another castle, on a high mountain in the land of Hiitola. Here stood a huge birch tree that reached to the skies, and on a branch of the tree sat a giant roasting an elk, which he held on the point of his lance over the fire. As soon as the giant saw Antti he called:

"Hurry, hurry, my lad, and I'll give you a dinner of roasted meat."

Antti was hungry, and gladly ate his fill. When he had finished the giant said: "Where are you going at such a pace?"

"I'm going to Louhi, to ask her a question."

"Ask her one for me, too. Ask her why I must needs sit in this tree all my life. Sometimes I am lucky enough to spear an elk but more often I nearly starve to death, for I'm held here a prisoner and cannot move."

"Surely I will ask her that," said Antti, and he leapt astride the black stallion again and hurried on his way.

At last he came to a wide river. By the shore was a little boat and in the boat an old woman, bent and toothless.

"If you will leave your horse here with me," said the old woman, "I will row you over to the other side. It is only a step from there to the castle of Louhi, and I'll be glad to show you the way."

[59]

"But shall I find my horse waiting for me when I come back?" Antti asked.

"If you bring me back an answer to my question from Louhi herself, I'll promise that your horse will be here waiting for you."

"Surely I will ask her your question," said Antti, and he stepped into the boat.

"Find out from Louhi," said the old woman as she bent over the creaking oars, "why I must be forever ferrying people across this river. For hundreds of years I've had to do this, and I am getting very tired."

Antii took the path which the old woman pointed out to him, and after a little while he came to tilled fields, and then a castle. He knocked at the door and the Daughter of the Rainbow, a lovely maiden with rosy cheeks, asked him in. Antti said:

"May I ask a few questions of Louhi, your mother?"

"My mother is not home today," the maiden answered, "but I expect her back at nightfall."

"I have come a long way," said Antti, "and I have many questions to ask. May I please wait here till your mother returns?"

The Daughter of the Rainbow looked at Antti's honest face and his kindly smile, and was curious to know what questions he had to ask. So Antti repeated them, one by one, and when he had finished she clapped her hands in laughter.

"O-ho, you want to know a great deal! But I'm afraid my mother will never answer all those questions for you."

Antti looked so sad at this that she added quickly: "Never mind, perhaps I can help you. When we hear Louhi coming, you must hide behind the cupboard. I will ask my mother the questions for you. Listen care-

[60]

fully, and then in the night you can slip out and hurry home again, without her being any the wiser."

By-and-by Louhi came home. When they heard her step, Antti crept behind the cupboard to listen.

"Did anyone come while I was gone?" asked Louhi as soon as she had opened the door.

"A man came early this morning with questions," answered her daughter, "but you were not at home, so I sent him on his way to ask elsewhere."

"O-ho! I could have told him anything he wanted to know," said Louhi. "What sort of questions did he ask?"

"He first asked in what trade a man would be happiest."

"He must have been a wise man to ask about happiness. I could have told him the old saying: Man is happiest when he plows the fields, clears the soil, piles the rocks in heaps, and plants seed that will grow into food for himself and his cattle."

"He also asked why the fruit belonging to a certain giant is always covered with mold."

"Only a fool would ask such a question! He should know that there lives a worm in the giant's garden that breathes upon the fruit. If the giant only has sense to crush this worm between two stones, his fruit will no longer be blighted."

"Another giant has lost the keys to his castle, and wants to know where to find them."

"How simple!" Louhi laughed contemptuously. "The giant will find his key fast enough if he looks between the stones leading to his own door."

"The man had still another question. A third giant has spent his life sitting fast in a birch tree, and wants to know how he can break his bonds."

[61]

"All he need do is to strike the foot of the tree with his lance. That will break the charm, and the limbs of the tree will fall to the ground and turn to pure gold."

"Last of all he wanted to know how the old woman who ferries people to and fro across the river may escape from her bondage."

"It's a pity the old woman is so stupid! All she has to do is to jump ashore when she next rows someone across, push the boat off with her left heel and repeat this charm:

Minä lähden tästä, sinä jäät siihen.

I leave here, you stay there.

Whoever happens to be in the boat at the time will then become the ferryman and the old woman will be free to do as she likes."

"Well, those were all the questions," said the Daughter of the Rainbow, with a ripple of laughter.

"The man must be a fool," Louhi said, "or he would have known the answers for himself. But if he ever comes back again, mind you don't tell them to him, for simple questions like these are considered the greatest secrets in the world of men."

When Louhi had finished, Antti felt so full of wisdom that he feared his head would burst with it all before he could get away. Time dragged, and it seemed a year before Louhi at last went to sleep. As soon as Antti heard her deep breathing, he crept from his hiding place, thanked the Daughter of the Rainbow, and ran back to the river.

"What did Louhi answer to my question?" the old woman wanted to know.

"I'll tell you as soon as you set me ashore on the opposite bank," Antti said.

When he had set foot on the sand he jumped astride his stallion and shouted:

Minä lähden tästa, sinä jäät siihen.

I leave here, you stay there.

This is Louhi's answer. You can work the charm on the next traveller who asks you to row him across!"

The old woman thanked Antti, and he rode away.

Soon he reached the giant who sat fidgeting in the birch tree, and told him Louhi's answer. The giant struck the foot of the tree with his lance, and to his surprise the branches fell to the ground and he with them. The fallen branches turned to pure gold and the giant was so happy that he gave Antti half of his riches to take with him.

Antti, riding happily on, met the next giant and told him where to find the keys of his castle. This giant was so glad that he gave Antti more gold.

As for the third giant, who carried the clouds upon his head, he was so happy to know how he could make his trees bear good fruit again that he gave Antti the stallion for his very own.

And now Antti rode like the wind back to the house of Ahnas, for he could scarcely wait to tell his wife, Alli, all his adventures and the good fortune that had befallen him.

When Ahnas saw that Antti had returned, he was furious. He said:

"Have you really been to Louhi, and has she truly told you in which trade a man is happiest?"

"These are Louhi's words," Antti replied. " 'Man is happiest when he plows the fields, clears the soil, piles the rocks in heaps, and plants seed that will grow into food for himself and his cattle.' "

This answer did not please Ahnas at all, for he hated to work or to stay in one place and besides, he was very greedy. He wanted to know at once where Antti had found all the gold that he brought home. And when Antti told him about his adventures, Ahnas made up his mind to set out himself on a journey through the land of Hiitola, and to ask Louhi how he might find more gold.

Antti offered to share his wealth. But the greedy merchant would not listen to him.

So Ahnas set off to visit Louhi. After a long journey, he at last came to the river where the old woman sat waiting in her boat. She rowed him across, then jumped ashore, gave the boat a shove with her left heel and said:

"I leave here, you stay there."

Then the charm fell upon Ahnas, and like it or not, he had to stay there in her stead.

Soon every man in Finland heard of Antti's great adventure and of Louhi's answer to the age-old question of mankind, how to find the greatest happiness, and from that time forth they became content to till the soil. For this reason Ahnas has had no passengers to row across the river to the land of Louhi, the ancient sorceress. From that day to this, he has remained in the boat.

And so the prophecy of the two wizards was fulfilled, for Antti fell heir to the merchant's estate and for many years lived happily with his gentle wife Alli.

LIPPO AND TAPIO

There was once a famous hunter named Lippo. All winter long he used to travel in search of game, and he was as much at home on his skiis as a bird is in the air.

One day Lippo and two of his friends set out to the Northland to hunt moose. All day long they followed tracks in the snow, but without meeting any game. At dusk they came to a small hut where they slept the night. Next morning they started out bright and early, again on their skiis. Lippo, who was setting the pace, kicked one ski against the other and said in fun:

"Today we must get a moose for each ski, and one for the ski-staff!"

New snow had fallen during the night, and presently sure enough they saw before them the fresh tracks of three large moose. They hastened their pace and soon caught up with two of the moose, who were fighting so hard that they paid no attention to the hunters. But the third moose saw them coming, and galloped off through the forest.

"Here's a piece of luck," whispered Lippo to his friends. "You shoot these two, and I will track down the third."

His friends killed the two moose and dragged them homeward, while Lippo swept forward on his skiis, light-hearted and alone. He flew swiftly over the snow, but however swiftly he travelled the tracks still stretched ahead of him, farther than his eyes could reach. At last, as night was falling, they led him through a fence and into a garden.

There, in the doorway of his house, stood Tapio, God of the Forests. His long beard was the color of moss and he wore a cap of leaves on his head. The moose, grunting with fright, stood beside him.

When Tapio saw Lippo he shouted angrily:

"How dare you hunt my moose, and drive him into a foaming sweat!"

"How could I tell he was your moose?" said Lippo. "He had strayed far into the forest."

When Tapio saw that Lippo was a plain, honest man his anger left him. He said:

"It is late and you are far from home. Come into my *tupa* and stay the night."

Lippo shook the snow from his skiis and set them up against the wall. When he followed the old man into the house, he was surprised to see the room crowded with

[66]

wild animals. Elk, bear, moose, wolf and fox, rabbit and weasel, there they all sat round the fire, talking each in his own tongue.

Tapio called in a loud voice like the sound of wind in the fir trees:

"Daughter! We have a guest!"

And there entered a lovely girl dressed in a robe of green leaves. She set a supper of honey, milk and bread on the birch-log table, and Lippo ate hungrily.

When he had eaten he turned to the girl, who was sitting now beside the fire, holding a fox in her arms, and asked her: "Who are you, and what is the name of this far north country?"

She answered: "I am Tellervo, daughter of Tapio, God of the Forests. My father takes care of every living creature in the woods. And this country is Pohjola, far to the north of your native Finland."

As darkness drew on and the first star came into the skies, the wild creatures began to file out into the forest, each to his own home. When the last had disappeared through the doorway, Tapio gave Lippo a bed of fir boughs beside the fire.

In the morning Lippo was up early, all ready to start out again in search of game, but nowhere could he find his skiis. They were gone as if by magic. When he asked Tapio what had happened to them the old man said:

"You will find them when you wish to go back to your own people. I have but one daughter, Tellervo. How would you like to stay here as my son-in-law?"

"I would gladly stay," said Lippo, "but I am only a poor man."

"*Ho* (Ho), don't let that worry you," Tapio said. "Lack of money is no crime. Here we need no gold."

So Lippo, the forest-wanderer, married Tellervo, and together they lived in the hut in the woods, with the old man, her father. Soon Lippo learned to speak the language of every creature living in the forest.

After three years a son was born to Lippo and Tellervo. Lippo was so proud that he wanted at once to go back to his family for a visit and tell them all the good news. He begged Tapio to go with him but Tapio said:

"First you must make me a pair of skiis. If the skiis are to my liking, then I will come with you."

Lippo went into the forest and began to hew out wood for the skiis. A little titmouse sat on a branch over his head, singing!

> Tii, tii, tiiainen,
> Vati, kuti, varpunen.

> Tit, tit, titmouse,
> Spicker, spacker, sparrow,
> Set the branch upon the shoulder,
> Form a head upon the foot-rest.

The titmouse made Lippo so fidgetty with its chirping that he did not even listen to what it said. He flung a stick at it and shouted: "Stop your noise, you chatterbox!"

Then he forgot all about the bird so intent was he on fashioning his skiis. He made them as beautifully as he knew how. And when at last they were finished, he brought them to his father-in-law. Tapio fastened the skiis to his feet and took a turn round the garden on them, saying: "These skiis are not for me. They don't fit me. You will have to make me a better pair."

Again Lippo went into the forest. And again the titmouse flew to a branch over his head and sang:

[68]

Tii, tii, tiiainen,
Vati, kuti, varpunen.

Tit, tit, titmouse,
Spicker, spacker, sparrow,
Set the branch upon the shoulder,
Form a head upon the foot-rest.

Again Lippo was very annoyed by this chattering. "Why must you be always chirping and chattering, you scamp!" he shouted, and this time he threw a chip of wood to frighten the bird away.

When the second pair of skiis were finished, Tapio tried them out and said: "These skiis are not for me, either. You'll have to keep on trying till you can do better."

Lippo went a third time into the forest, determined to please his father-in-law. And a third time the titmouse sang:

Tii, tii, tiiainen,
Vati, kuti, varpunen.

This time Lippo stood listening.

"What are you trying to tell me, you little fidget? I'll try your advice. You can't be singing the same thing over and over for no reason at all."

He worked fast, and did as the bird said. In the center of the ski he fashioned a shoulder for Tapio to stand upon. He bent the front end of the ski slightly upward into a head, so that it would glide more easily over the snow.

When Tapio tried this new pair of skiis he was delighted.

"*Ka*, these are the skiis for me! They fit me perfectly.

[69]

You must have learned at last to listen to the words of your little forest friends, my Lippo, or you would never have known how to please me. Now you may go home!"

So they started, Tapio first, Lippo with his child strapped to his back, and Tellervo his wife close behind him.

When they had gone far into the deep wild forest Tapio stopped and said: "From now on I shall travel ahead of you. Follow my tracks in the snow. Each time you see the hole of my pointed ski-staff, there make your camp for the night. Weave the roof of your lodge carefully of fir boughs, and be sure that no light from the stars can shine through to work you harm."

And he set off ahead like a flash of light on his skiis, and was gone.

All day long Lippo followed the ski tracks, with Tellervo and his child. Night was falling when they saw the first hole made by Tapio's staff. Here they found a moose broiled and steaming for their supper.

Lippo built a lodge as Tapio had told him. He wove the fir branches carefully so that no starlight could shine through. He took the birch bark pack from his shoulders and set his child in the lodge before the fire. Here they all three slept the night.

In the morning they ate again, took enough moose meat for a meal during the day, and set out to follow Tapio's ski tracks.

Again at nightfall they saw the second hole made by Tapio's staff. Beside it was a deer roasted and steaming. They ate, built a lodge of fir boughs as before, and slept the night.

The third day they pushed forward on their skiis, and at nightfall found only a wood grouse fried and steaming. They were so hungry that no morsel remained for next day's meal.

Lippo was greatly disheartened. He said:

"Tellervo, we cannot travel without food. My bow and arrows I left in the hut. Tapio and his magic have failed us, and my home is still far away."

That night he took no heed how he built their lodge. He wove the fir boughs carelessly, and through the bare chinks the starlight shone through on them.

In the morning when Lippo rose to stir the camp fire, he found that his wife, Tellervo, was gone. Far and near Lippo searched, but he could not find her. He asked the birds in the trees where she had gone but, when they answered him, he found he could no longer understand their language.

He went into the hut and took his child upon his knee. Sad and hopeless he sat there before the fire. He saw moose and deer outside in the forest but he had no weapons to hunt them.

The next morning and the next and the next, every morning when he awoke, Lippo found a wood grouse cooked and steaming before the door. Many years passed, and still Lippo lived in his lodge of fir boughs before the open fire in the forest. He dreamed of home, but he no longer had courage to set out on the search for it.

Lippo's son grew into a tall boy, and from boyhood he grew to manhood. He asked Lippo to teach him about the stars, so that he could travel alone and learn more about the world.

One day when he came back from exploring the forest he said: "Father, we are not far from your home. To the south lie your home fields."

[71]

Then he took his father, who was now an old man, and together they set out on the journey. After a day's travel they found themselves at Lippo's old home. Tears came to Lippo's eyes at the sight of his old country after all these years, but the boy was not content to stay there. He left his father behind and travelled north once more to make a home for himself.

And to this very day the Laplanders proudly trace their descent from this wise and restless son of Lippo, the mighty hunter.

THE WOOING OF SEPPO ILMARINEN

Seppo Ilmarinen stood at his anvil in the smithy, beating out a piece of red hot iron. Clang, clang, went his hammer. He looked up, and there before him stood a queer little woman, as tiny as a dwarf. Just like a jointed wooden doll she looked, and her movements were quick and jerky. And she piped up in a voice like the chirping of a cricket:

"If you knew what I know, Seppo Ilmarinen, you wouldn't stand there hammering iron!"

"And what is it you know?" said Seppo. "If it's good news I'll give you my blessing, but if it's bad news all you get is a curse!"

"What I say is the truth," returned the little woman. "At this very moment there are two suitors rowing in boats to Hiitola. They are after the hand of Katrina, the King's daughter, and no less!"

When he heard this Seppo dropped his hammer on the floor, shut up his blacksmith shop and rushed home as fast as his legs would carry him.

"Aiti, Aiti," he shouted to his mother, "build a fire in the *sauna*, quick. Make the water sizzle on the bath-house stones! Give me a clean shirt and new bark shoes!"

When he had taken his bath he shouted to his servant:

"Catch the three-year-old colt, and put the iron harness on him with the new reins. Hitch him up to the painted sledge."

The servant harnessed the colt, but the colt was so wild that it took the two of them to get him between the shafts. He kicked and he plunged as Seppo gathered up the reins.

"Give me your blessing, Mother," Seppo cried. "I'm going a-wooing!"

"I bless you indeed," called his mother. "May no charm come near you to work you harm!"

Seppo went swishing along over the open sea in his painted sledge, with the wild colt pulling it. He flew so fast that no wave touched him, and the sledge runners left no track in the water. After a long time he caught up with the two suitors in their boats. So the queer little woman had told him the truth! They were on their way to woo the beautiful Katrina. Seppo shouted a greeting to them, and together they hurried on.

The beautiful Katrina was sitting before the castle, on the third terrace of the King's garden, looking out across the sea. When she saw the three specks on the water she called to her old nurse.

"See, nurse, my three suitors are coming! Two are rowing in boats, but the third one comes in a sledge."

[74]

When the three suitors reached the castle door, the King greeted them kindly. He gave them meat and drink. When they had eaten the three young men knelt before the King and said:

"Noble King, we have come to pay court to your beautiful daughter, Katrina."

The King replied: "Answer me this question. Which of you can plow my field of snakes, with unshod feet and unbound ankles?"

When the two suitors who had come by boat heard these words, they were very much upset. They stammered their excuses and went their ways. But Seppo stood bravely before the King and said:

"I will plow your field of snakes barefoot, if that is your wish."

"Good," said the King. "My servants will show you the field."

Seppo hitched his wild colt to the King's plow, took off his shoes and set to work. When the snakes saw him coming they reared high on their tails and hissed, striking with their poisonous fangs. But Seppo whispered to his colt, and they ran so fast that the snakes flew beneath the plowshare and over his head, but not one touched him.

"O King," said Seppo, "your field is plowed."

"You've made a good beginning," said the King, "But now I want you to make a sparkling pool in my garden, where big fish may swim and small fish flicker and glitter in the sun. And this you must do not with tools, but by the power of song alone."

"It shall be as you wish," said Seppo.

He walked straightway into the garden, and there he sang a brave song.

Luonotar, oi Ilman Neiti,

Luonotar, Lady of Creation,
Grant me the power of winged song.
Sparkle water in the pool,
Flicker minnows in the sun.

And by magic there lay a sparkling pool where a moment ago had been smooth green grass. He could plainly see the large fish swimming and the silver flicker of the darting minnows. Again Seppo stood before the King.

"O King, my task is done. There lies your pool and there swim your fishes."

The King looked kindly at Seppo, and said: "You have indeed made a good beginning. But there is one thing more you must do. My daughter has need of the *Huomenlahja Lipas,* the hope chest which has long lain hidden under the sea. Bring her this, and you shall have her hand in marriage."

"It shall be as you wish," Seppo answered.

With a strong heart he strode forth from the King's palace, and soon reached the sea shore. Here he saw three strange women, robed in green seaweed. They were sitting on the shore, sifting the sand through their long fingers. Seppo called to them:

"O maidens, where is the *huomenlahja lipas* for the beautiful Katrina? Tell me where it lies hidden under the waves."

"To find that," answered the maidens, "you must go to Ukko Untamoinen, the sleepy old man of the sea who keeps all dreams hidden from mortal eyes. You can just see his *tupa* across the waves. Go and ask him, but be sure to keep your wits about you. For many have gone to Ukko, but few have returned."

Seppo hurried on to the hut of the old man of the sea, there he looked in through the window. There lay Ukko Untamoinen, the great drowsy giant, stretched out along the floor sound asleep. He was so big that his feet and head stuck out through the doorway and his body filled the whole *tupa*. Seppo jumped over the old man's feet and into the hut. He shouted:

"Ukko Untamoinen, give me the hidden hope chest for my beautiful Katrina."

Ukko Untamoinen rubbed his eyes with his huge green fists drowsily, and said:

"First you must climb up and dance on my tongue, so that it tickles. Then I will give you the hope chest."

The giant stuck out his great tongue as he spoke, and Seppo climbed up on it and began to dance. But no sooner had he begun to dance than Ukko opened his huge mouth wide and tilted his head, and Seppo went tumbling headlong down into his belly. The drowsy giant smiled, and closed his eyes again. He had finished with Seppo.

But Seppo had not finished with him. Instead of being frightened, Seppo kept his wits about him. He drew from his shirt a forge, and from his sleeve a bellows; from his right boot a pair of tongs and from his left boot a great hammer. He rolled up his sleeves and he started to work. From his bosom he drew forth a piece of copper. This he heated in his forge and hammered out a bird with hard claws and a sharp pointed beak. Then Seppo sang one of his brave songs, and blew into the copper bird the breath of life. The bird tore with its claws and beak, and flapped with its wings, and soon the drowsy old man of the sea was doubled up with pain. He clutched at his belly and cried to Seppo:

[77]

"If you'll only come out of my belly I'll give you the hope chest!"

Seppo climbed out on the giant's tongue once more, and jumped to the ground.

"Go back to the sea shore," Ukko Untamoinen grumbled. "You will see there three maidens sifting sand between their fingers. Repeat this charm, and they will tell you where the chest is hidden:

> Ukko Untamoisen onnella.
> By the luck of Ukko Untamoinen.

Seppo found the three maidens again. They were sifting sand through their fingers.

"O good maidens," he called to them, "give me the hope chest which you guard for my beautiful Katrina. Ukko Untamoinen promised it to me . . . Ukko Untamoisen onnella."

"Here it is, hidden under the sand," the maidens answered, "and very glad we are that you've come to fetch it. We are tired of guarding it."

Seppo dug through the sand and uncovered the hope chest. Then he hoisted it to his shoulder, hurrying back to the King's palace.

"Here, King," he said, "is the *huomenlahja lipas* which you sent me to seek for Katrina."

When the King saw that Seppo had brought the chest he was satisfied at last. Sending for the fair rosy-cheeked Katrina, he gave her to Seppo for his wife, with his blessing upon them both.

Seppa once more harnessed his wild colt with the iron harness and the stout reins and started out with Katrina in the painted sledge, swishing across the open sea. The wild colt flew so fast that no wave touched them, and the sledge runners left no track on the water.

[78]

Hard they drove, till night overtook them in the midst of the sea. Then Seppo sang a brave song, and by the magic of his song there rose a beautiful island before them. Here they stopped for the night.

With the coming of dawn Seppo awoke. He looked about him, but nowhere could he see Katrina. She had disappeared. He looked here, he looked there, and saw only the wild ducks circling in the air. He counted them and found there was one duck too many. So he sang:

"Do not try to hide, Katrina, I have found you."

At once one of the wild ducks turned into a fair rosy-cheeked girl, and Katrina stood before him, smiling. Seppo took Katrina into his painted sledge and once more they drove across the open sea. When night overtook them Seppo sang another brave song, and again an island rose before them.

Again, when Seppo awoke in the morning, there was no Katrina. He searched the island, and counted all the trees. There was one tree too many. He sang:

"Do not try to hide, Katrina, I have found you."

And when the trees heard his song, one of them stepped forth, and there stood Katrina.

The third day Seppo took Katrina once more into his painted sledge, and once more they drove across the sea. When night overtook them, he sang a third time, and a third time an island rose before them. When day dawned Seppo awoke and saw that his Katrina was once more missing.

This time he grew hot with anger.

"No more shall Katrina deceive me!" he shouted.

He counted the rocks along the shore, and found that there was one rock too many.

[79]

"Do not hide, Katrina, I have found you," he called.

But when Katrina stood before him, he said with a bitter heart:

"Long have I paid court to you, Katrina. For the King, your father, I have done many tasks, and is this my pay, that you should deceive and mock me? For this you shall live forever upon the sea. I will make you into a tern, and every day shall you fly against the wind."

Then he sang a brave song, and as he sang Katrina turned into a gray bird and flew away.

But as he saw her flying away upon the wind Seppo grew sad. His heart was empty. He felt that he could not live alone. So he set up his forge, drew a piece of copper from his breast, and began to hammer out a woman to suit his fancy. And when he had finished he sang a brave song, and there came into the copper the breath of life.

At first Seppo was pleased with this woman of his own handiwork. She obeyed him in everything. But soon he grew tired of being obeyed. He grew tired of his cold copper woman and cast her away.

After long days of wandering and loneliness, Seppo heard a soft knocking within his heart. A voice said:

"I am wisdom. Listen to me, and know the truth. A man should not try to make a woman after his own dreams. He should learn to be happy with the wife Hiisi has given him."

Then Seppo sang his brave song for the last time. And as he sang a gray sea-bird swooped down beside him, and there stood his wife, Katrina.

Seppo wasted no time. He took Katrina into his painted sledge, whipped up his wild colt, and with laughter in his heart swept homeward.

JURMA AND THE SEA GOD

There was once a farmer named Jurma, who lived by the sea. One hot day while he was plowing in the fields he grew tired, so he sat down on the rocks and dangled his feet in the cool waves to rest them.

While he was sitting there a Sea God caught him by the ankles and said:

"Unless you give me your eldest daughter, Impi, I will drag you under the water and drown you."

The farmer tried to kick the Sea God's long scaly fingers from his ankles but the more he struggled the tighter the Sea God held on.

"I have never harmed you," begged the farmer. "Let me go. I love Impi too much to give her to you."

"All right," laughed the Sea God as he gave Jurma's ankles another tug. "Come yourself, then."

[81]

Jurma was very frightened as he clutched at the rocks.

"Let me go, let me go," he cried, "and I will give you my daughter!"

As Jurma spoke, the Sea God let go of his ankles, and for one moment stood up in the water. The green scales of his body glittered in the sun as he said:

"You must not forget your promise."

Then he dived under the waters and was gone.

When Jurma reached his *tupa* he dared not tell his wife what had happened. He simply said:

"Impi, I forgot to bring the horse's reins from the rocks where I was resting. Run and fetch them for me, for I'm very tired."

Impi did as he told her, and ran gaily down to the shore. The Sea God, who was waiting under the water, saw her standing there on the rocks. He caught her in his long green arms and carried her off to his palace under the waves. When he came to his sea kingdom, he set Impi on her feet again and knelt before her. And he said a charm:

> Kultani kallihin,
> Minum Sydämeni sinulle,
> Sinun sydämesi minulle.

> Golden, one, priceless one,
> My heart to you, yours to me.

And at once Impi fell in love with the Sea God.

At first Impi was so dazed by the world under the sea that she thought she was dreaming. All about her was a blue haze. In the Sea King's palace the chairs and tables were made of finest green coral, and the walls of flowing green tapestry. The door yard of the palace was planted with great fronds of waving sea weeds, and paved with all kinds of shells. Strangest of all was the fence of shining eels that enclosed the castle.

"Here we shall be at home," said the Sea God. "You are now my wife and shall rule my palace as you choose."

Impi smiled, for she loved the Sea God, but she longed for the light of the sun and the stars, for the sweet clean air of the upper world. The green shadows amused her, but she still felt strange and lonely.

Years passed, and Impi grew used to this strange world under the waters. But the Sea God became restless and wanted to go away for a time. One day he said to Impi:

"I must make a long journey, and shall be gone for many days. Here are the keys to all the chambers of the palace. Amuse yourself until my return. You can do anything you like, and go anywhere you wish, only do not enter the last chamber at the back of the palace. This is my private room, and no one ever crosses its threshold but myself."

After the Sea God had gone, Impi wandered through the palace from room to room. She opened and closed every door a dozen times, and at length became curious to enter the Sea God's private chamber.

"My husband will never know, if I enter his chamber," she said to herself, "but what would it matter, even if he did!"

She put the great key into the lock and drew it out again two or three times to see if anything would happen. Then she put her ears to the keyhole each time, but all was silent.

When Impi entered the room, she was surprised to see only bare, dingy walls. There was a wide shelf and two large bottles. In the center of the floor stood a huge keg filled with black tar, and on top of the tar floated a beautiful golden ring. Impi tried the ring on her finger, and as she did so, a large drop of tar touched her hand and burned like fire.

Impi was frightened, and threw the ring back into the tar. She ran out of the room, and locked the door behind her. She tried to rub the tar stain from her finger and to ease the burn. But the more she rubbed, the blacker the stain became, and the more it pained her.

That evening the Sea God returned, tired with his journey and glad to be at home.

"Impi," he said, "take my head in your lap, and lay your hands on my brow to ease my headache."

When Impi's stained finger touched the Sea God's forehead, he leapt to his feet and cried:

"What is that, a coal of fire on my brow?"

"I have no fire in my hands," said Impi, holding out her palms to him.

Then the Sea God saw the stain on Impi's finger, and said angrily:

"You have tricked me. I gave you the keys to every room in the palace, and you have gone into my secret chamber."

Impi begged for mercy, but the Sea God was furious. He carried her into the secret chamber, and threw her into the great keg of tar.

While all these things were happening under the sea, Impi's father continued to dwell with his wife and his two remaining daughters on the sea-shore. One day while Impi's father was fishing in his boat in the bay, the boat caught on the sand. He tried in every way to free it, but the boat would not move. While he was pushing with his oar, the Sea God lifted his shining green head above the water, and said, smiling:

"My good man, this is not the first time I have met you. Give me your second daughter, Hella, and I will set you free."

"Cruel Sea God!" shouted Jurma. "Have you no pity? Haven't you already harmed me enough?"

But as he spoke, his boat began to sink.

"I have a beautiful palace, and Hella will be very happy," said the Sea God. "Make haste and decide, for your boat is already shipping water."

The father began to weep. "Save me, and I'll give you my daughter!"

"Very well, I will be waiting at the shore," said the Sea God and he dived under the waves.

When Hella's father reached his *tupa,* he could not bear to tell what had happened. He simply said:

"Hella, I have forgot my fishing spear in the boat. Fetch it to me."

Hella ran down to the boat, whereupon the Sea God seized her, and carried her quickly under the water to his palace.

Years passed, and the Sea God decided to go on another journey. He gave his keys to Hella and said:

"While I am gone, you may do as you like. You may have the freedom of the entire palace, but do not enter my private chamber."

When he had left, Hella too became curious, and entered the chamber. She tried on the ring as her sister had done, and stained her finger. When the Sea God returned, he threw Hella, too, into the keg of tar.

In the Upper World, time had passed slowly for Hella's father and mother, and for the younger sister, Vieno. The father had learned his lesson, and stayed away from the sea. When his wife and daughter asked

him to bring them fish, he always found some excuse.
But one day, after his wife had begged him to set his nets
on the shallow sand at low tide, he went down to the
shore.

As he approached his boat, he saw a pair of the most
finely woven birch bark shoes he had ever seen. He decided to try them on his feet.

No sooner were the shoes on his feet, than they began
to slide with him toward the water. He realized too late
that the shoes were bewitched, for when he tried to kick
them off, they carried him quickly into the waves. He
was in the water up to his waist, then up to his neck.

As he struggled, there stood the Sea God beside him,
smiling.

"Is there nothing I can do for you, my good man?"

"Free me from these cursed birch bark shoes," cried
Jurma. "They are carrying me to a watery grave."

"This should teach you not to take what does not belong to you," laughed the Sea God. "Now you are in
my power, and unless you give me your third daughter,
Vieno, I will not help you."

The father was now broken-hearted, and begged for
mercy.

"Your Vieno will be happier with me," said the Sea
God, "than she is with you. I shall give her every treasure that her heart wishes."

When the father went back to his *tupa* he said wearily:

"Vieno, I have forgotten my birch bark shoes on the
shore beside the boat. Fetch them to me."

Vieno feared nothing, and ran happily down to the
water. The Sea God caught her in his arms, and carried
her joyfully away to his green shadowed palace. He gave
her of his wealth and jewels, and at last she became ac-

customed to the strange, dreamy land under the sea.

One day the Sea God said to Vieno:

"My dear wife, I am going on a long journey. Here are the keys to my palace. You are welcome to enter every room but one . . ."

When he had gone, Vieno entered the forbidden chamber, as her sisters had done, and looked cautiously about her, for she suspected some sort of trickery.

She examined the two large bottles on the shelf. One was labelled THE WATER OF LIFE, and the other THE WATER OF DEATH.

Then she noticed the keg and the golden ring floating on the top of the thick black tar. She looked closely at the tar, and suddenly discovered the eyes of her two sisters staring coldly at her.

Vieno was weak with fright. She wondered what she could do. She remembered, then, the Water of Life, and lifted the great bottle down from the shelf.

She sprinkled the Water of Life upon the tar, and when she had shaken the last drop from the bottle, there stood her two sisters before her, rubbing their eyes as if awakened from a bad dream.

Vieno then poured all the Water of Death into the bottle labelled the Water of Life, and placed the two bottles again on the shelf. When she told her sisters all that had happened, she led them from the terrible secret chamber, and locked the door.

For a time the three sisters stood, trembling with fear lest the Sea God should return and find them. They thought hard, and finally decided upon a plan of escape. Vieno placed Impi and Hella in two large sea chests, and fastened them securely.

When the Sea God returned, Vieno said sweetly:

[87]

"My lord, you look tired, and your hair and beard are tangled. Lay your head upon my knees, and I will bring my golden comb."

This pleased the Sea God, and as she smoothed his temples, and ran the comb through his hair, he grew gentle and said:

"My dear wife, is there not something I can do to make you happy?"

"I have been wondering," said Vieno, "if you would mind doing a little errand for me. My parents are poor, while we have plenty and to spare. Will you not carry this sea chest, and place it on the shore by their *tupa* where they will find it? I had rather you would not open it, for I am ashamed to have you see the women's trifles that I am sending to my mother."

The Sea God laughed, but took the sea chest upon his shoulder, and set it down before Jurma's *tupa*.

When the Sea God returned, Vieno again took his head upon her knees until he became gentle.

"I know it has made you happy to carry the sea chest to my parents. Will you not make two more journeys for me? The chests are so small, and my parents are so sorely in need, that three chests will be little to pay for all that I owe them. Do these errands for me, and I shall never ask you another favor."

The Sea God gladly took the second chest, in which was hidden Hella, and set it down on the sand before Jurma's *tupa*.

While he was gone, Vieno gathered many treasures together into the third chest. Then she made a dummy of pillows, and dressed it in her own clothes. This she set upon the balcony where the Sea God would see it upon his return.

[88]

Vieno then climbed into the third chest, and clamped down the lid. When she heard the Sea God coming, she said in a loud voice:

"Carry this third chest at once to my parents without opening it, and they will be very grateful for the good turn you have done them."

The Sea God peered upward through the green shadows, and saw the figure upon the balcony. He thought it was his Vieno, and so he took the third chest upon his shoulders and started off. After he had gone a little way he set the chest down.

"This chest is so heavy," he said to himself, "that I must see what it contains before I go any farther."

"Do not look inside," called a strange voice. "Did you not promise me that?"

"She can still see me," said the Sea God. "That is why she climbed up to the balcony, so that she could watch what I am doing."

Again he struggled a long time under his burden, and again set the sea chest down to open it. But a strange voice, half in a whisper, said:

"Do not deceive me. Remember your promise. Do not look inside, but keep on your way."

"Never again will I go on an errand for my wife," swore the Sea God as he again set out. "She is too clever."

As soon as he had set the third chest upon the sand, he returned in high spirits. He entered his castle shouting:

"Hurry the dinner, for I have a ravenous appetite."

He looked up at the silent dummy upon the balcony. He started up the steps at a bound, saying:

"Something must have happened to Vieno, that she does not move or answer."

[89]

When he saw how he had been tricked, he struck at the dummy in his anger, but lost his balance, and tumbled headlong down the stairs. The Sea God was so badly bruised that he went to his secret chamber, and taking down the bottle labelled THE WATER OF LIFE, drank deeply. But, alas, this was the Water of Death, and so the Sea God never knew what happened.

In the farmer's *tupa* there was great rejoicing when Jurma and his wife found their three daughters in the chests upon the shore. They sold the treasures and jewels that Vieno had brought with her, and forever after had plenty, and to spare.

And now that the Sea God had come to his well-deserved end, there was no one left to spoil their happiness.

TIMO AND THE PRINCESS VENDLA

There was once a proud King who had an only daughter named Vendla. He said:

"My daughter shall be different from any other woman in the world. I want her to be wiser than anyone else, in order that she will do me honor."

So he sent for all the most famous teachers, and told them to teach his daughter every language in the world. After Vendla had learned French and English and German and Spanish and Greek and Latin and Chinese and all the other languages as well, so that she could talk to the courtiers of the world each in his own tongue, the King called his heralds and said:

"Go forth throughout the whole kingdom, and say to the people: 'The King will give the Princess Vendla in marriage to the man who can speak a new tongue that she does not understand. But let everyone beware, for any man who dares to woo the Princess without speaking a new tongue shall be flung into the Baltic Sea.' "

It happened that there dwelt in the kingdom a young shepherd lad named Timo. Timo was a dreamer who spent his time wandering about the deep wild forest talking to the birds and the beasts. And by talking to them he had learned to understand their language, and they his.

When Timo heard the King's proclamation he laughed.

"It shouldn't be so hard to win the Princess Vendla. There are many tongues in the world. Even the wisest men and women cannot understand them all."

So he started on his way to the King's castle. Before he had gone very far he met a sparrow.

"Where are you going with such a happy face, Timo?" the sparrow chirped.

"I am going to marry the Princess Vendla. Come with me and I'll give you a ride in my fine leather pouch."

"Surely I'll go with you," said the sparrow. And he hopped into the pouch, while Timo went his way.

Presently Timo met a squirrel that sat under his fluffy tail and nibbled at a hazelnut.

"Where are you going with such a happy face, Timo?" chattered the squirrel.

"I am going to marry the learned Princess Vendla."

"How wonderful!"

"Come with me and I'll give you a ride in my fine leather pouch."

The squirrel hopped into the pouch, and Timo strode gaily onward. Soon he met a crow, then a raven, then an owl. Each in turn asked him where he was going, and each in turn hopped into Timo's leather pouch to keep him company. On he strode, and before he knew it he came to the gates of the King's castle.

"Halt! Who are you?" boomed one of the King's soldiers.

"I am Timo, and I've come to woo the fair and learned Princess Vendla."

"Why, you're only a shepherd boy," cried the guard. "What's more, you're a fool as well."

"You must be in a hurry to taste the Baltic Sea!" laughed another of the soldiers.

"You can't even speak your own tongue properly, let alone others," cried a third soldier. "Where you come from, the people all talk as if they had a hot potato in their mouth!"

"You'd better run along back to your flocks while you've still got a chance," added the first soldier.

But Timo stood his ground.

"I come to woo the most beautiful and learned Princess Vendla," he said again. "Open the gates and let me in, for I can speak a dozen tongues that the Princess has never even heard."

"Well, remember we warned you," said the guard as he slowly opened the gates. "Next thing you know, we'll be giving you a ride to the Baltic Sea!"

Vendla was seated beside her father on a high golden throne. Her hair was decked with jewels and her face was so beautiful that when Timo saw her he fell on his knees.

"Is it true, most beautiful and learned Princess, that you will marry the man who can speak a language you do not understand?"

"This must be a brave man," thought the Princess as she looked at Timo standing there with his leather pouch across his shoulder.

"Yes," she said, "it is true."

[93]

"Do you know what will happen to you if you dare to woo the Princess, and fail to speak this unknown tongue you talk about?" thundered the King.

"I would swim a dozen seas bigger than the Baltic for such a Princess," cried Timo as he looked into Vendla's blue eyes.

"Then let us hear this fine language of yours," said the King.

Timo turned to the Princess.

"Listen, most beautiful Princess, and tell me if you understand."

As he spoke Timo thrust his hand into the leather pouch, and touched the sparrow softly. The bird woke up and chirped:

"*Tshiu, tshiu, tshiu, tshiu!* What do you want, Timo?"

"What tongue is that?" Timo asked.

"Truly," said the Princess, "it is a language I have never heard."

"So you don't understand all the tongues in the world!" Timo laughed. He touched the squirrel's tail.

"*Rak-rak-rak! Rak-rak! Ka-ka-ka-ka-ka-ka!* Leave me alone!" chattered the squirrel.

"Do you understand that?" Timo asked.

"I do not," said the Princess meekly.

Then Timo touched the crow.

"*Vaak, vaak, vaak—ak-ak!* Don't disturb me!" cawed the crow.

The Princess shook her head in amazement. Neither could she understand the *"thiuu, thiuu, thiuu"* of the woodpecker, nor the *"kronk, kronk, kronk"* of the raven.

"It is all most strange," said the Princess. "I cannot understand why my teachers never taught me these words!"

"You see, there are many languages that even the wisest men on earth do not know," said Timo, smiling.

"Vendla, I thought you the most learned woman in the world," cried the King furiously, "yet you let a country lad make fools of us both!"

"O King, this is not so," Timo pleaded. "Vendla is still the most learned lady in the land, for she has admitted her ignorance, and truly the greatest wisdom is to know that one does not know everything."

The Princess was pleased with Timo's honest eyes and his understanding words. She was glad that he had won her hand.

"O King," asked Timo, "will you now keep your bargain with me?"

"Take Vendla for your bride," answered the King. "You have won her, and with her I give you the half of my kingdom. May you always be as wise in the future as you have shown yourself today!"

Then the Princess climbed down from her high throne, and Timo took her in his arms and kissed her cheek.

The King proclaimed a glorious holiday with feasting throughout the land, and Timo and Vendla lived happily ever after.

SEVERI AND VAPPU

There was a young man named Severi who set out one spring morning to find his fortune.

The sun shone, the birds sang, and Severi felt so light-hearted that he too sang for joy, and so eager that his feet fairly ran away with him. Over hills and meadows, through deep woods he wandered, until at last he came to the wide ocean, where he saw a little rowboat dancing on the tide.

"Now I will sail to some far country," cried Severi. "Who knows what adventures I may meet!"

So he jumped into the little boat and set forth. For many days and nights Severi battled against waves and tide, but he was young and strong and he feared nothing. Then one day a great wind began to blow and a black storm beat down upon him. The rain fell in sheets, the thunder and lightning flashed and rumbled. All at once a huge wave swept over Severi's head and hurled him into the water.

But still Severi did not lose heart. He swam day and night, until at last the tide washed him upon a shining white beach at the foot of a tall black cliff. Severi saw a rope hanging over the edge of the cliff. He caught hold of the rope and climbed hand over hand until he reached the top. There before him lay a new strange country, with distant icy mountains glittering in the sun.

After he had rested for a while, Severi noticed a little path which ran along the edge of the cliff and between the hills. In and out it wound, and Severi followed it, until presently it led him to a stairway that went deep into the very heart of the black cliff.

Severi walked down and down the stone steps until he thought he must have reached the very center of the earth. There at the bottom was a golden door. He lifted his hand to knock, but as he did so the door swung open all by itself and Severi stepped through. There he stood in a wonderful world of green meadows with beautiful flowers and shining trees all laden with golden fruit.

In the distance rose the turrets of a copper castle, shining like red gold in the sun. Straight to the castle Severi walked, and stood before it wondering. As he gazed and wondered, suddenly he saw an old man standing beside him, with glittering white hair. He was a strange old man, but Severi saw that his cheeks were young.

"Where are you travelling, my boy?" the old man asked him.

"That is not easy to say," Severi answered. "First I wandered for days across mountain and valley and woodland. Then I rowed on the broad blue back of the ocean. A storm overturned my boat and I swam for many days. At last the tide washed me up on the sands at the foot of your cliff, and here I am."

"*Ka!*" laughed the old man. "Since you have come so far, why not stay here? If you like, you can be my servant."

"It is a bargain," cried Severi. "I ask nothing better."

So the old man took Severi into his shining copper castle. There he gave him food fit for the gods—all that he could eat and more. When at length Severi rose from the table, the old man said:

"Here are the keys to my castle. There are twenty-four rooms and twenty-four keys. You may use every key and open every room except one. The twenty-fourth room you enter at your own risk. If ever you unlock that door I will not be to blame for anything that may happen to you."

"Good," said Severi, already beginning to feel very curious.

Next day the old man set out on a long journey, and Severi was left all alone in the great copper castle. He said to himself:

"I have twenty-three rooms to explore. I know that each will be filled with a different wonder."

He took the first key and, turning it in the first lock, threw open the first gleaming door. At once his eyes were so dazzled he thought the whole room was on fire. Then he saw that the room and everything in it was of new, shining copper. The sun, pouring through the window and striking on the walls and floor and tables and chairs, nearly blinded him.

All this was fine, but it was not adventure, and it was adventure that Severi sought. So he turned the second key in the lock. The second room was all of heavy silver. This, too, so dazzled his eyes that he rushed to see what the third room was like. Here the walls were all of purest leaf gold, but their glitter so nearly blinded him that he hurried on to the other rooms, each in turn.

One of the rooms was of black ebony, one of warm Italian marble. One seemed to be cut from the heart of a cold green emerald, another from topaz and still another from red garnet. There was a room of blue sapphire and one of lapis lazuli.

After gazing on so many wonders Severi began to grow tired and hungry and thirsty. He wished he were back in his native *tupa* with his bed of straw and his supper of black bread.

The next door opened into a room of mother-of-pearl. Severi felt as though he were standing in the middle of a great gleaming sea-shell. On the floor stood a carved couch covered with the softest silk. Severi stepped eagerly toward it but the silk covers were so smooth and beautiful that he dared not lay hands upon them.

A little sadly Severi walked to the door of the next room. When he had flung it open, he saw a table of gold laden with strange fruits. Some gave forth a golden fragrance and some were transparent as emerald. There were red berries with the fresh dew still upon them. But they were so perfect Severi was afraid to touch them.

There was a beaker of sparkling wine, too, and some of this Severi poured into a crystal goblet. But when he lifted the glass the sun from the window filled it with such a strange and lovely light that he feared to drink.

And now Severi grew sad, for he knew that he had entered every one of the three and twenty rooms.

"What is there left for me?" he thought. "All my adventures are over and done."

Turning back now, like one in a dream he laid a hand on the fruit and ate it, and he drank the wine at a single gulp. And suddenly he felt very weary. He thought of the silken couch, and throwing himself down upon it he fell into a heavy sleep.

When he awoke, he found that the key to the twenty-fourth room was clasped in his hand. Severi began looking at it curiously, turning over in his mind what might happen if he opened the twenty-fourth door.

"What can there be in this last room?" he wondered. "I think I shall open it and find out. I don't believe anything very terrible will happen. . . . The old man didn't really forbid me to open the door. He only said I would enter at my own risk."

Bravely he set the twenty-fourth key into the lock, and threw open the heavy door.

There in the middle of the room, on a high throne, sat the loveliest maid in all the world. Her eyes were as blue as the deepest sea, her hair shone golden like the sun, and her smile was like the warm red south.

For a time Severi could only stare and stare. Then at last he said in a soft whisper. "What is your name?"

"Vappu," answered the maiden, her voice like the rippling music of a *kantele*.

"And why do you sit here?"

"For a very good reason. So far no one has ever come to take me away."

"Would you leave your throne if you could?" Severi asked, gaining courage as he spoke.

"It has been told in an old prophecy," said Vappu, "that whoever should open the door of this room, with him should I go and to him alone should I belong."

Proudly Severi stepped forward and held out his hand. Vappu placed her soft fingers within his as he helped her down, then she whispered:

[100]

"I have been waiting for you a very long time, *kultani*."

Days and nights passed as in a dream, while Vappu and Severi dwelt together in the copper castle. The new moon rose and waned, and not once did they think of the old man, who was still away on his journey.

One day after they had eaten their noon-day meal Vappu led Severi into a deep orchard where cool winds swept through the swaying boughs. Red and golden birds sang among the trees. A brook rippled in the sunlight and beside its clear waters blossomed the Tree of Life.

Severi and Vappu sat beneath the Tree of Life. They ate of its golden fruit and drank from the sparkling brook beside it.

After a while Severi fell into a deep sleep. When at last he awoke and opened his eyes, Vappu was gone.

Severi was frightened. In and out between the trees he ran, calling: "Vappu, Vappu, Vappu!" But the only sound he could hear was the song of the red and golden birds that flittered among the branches.

For a long while Severi searched and called. He ran in and out of the twenty-four doors of the castle crying over and over again: "Vappu, Vappu, Vappu!"

But only the echo of his own voice mocked him, and the sound of his own footsteps.

Again and again Severi searched the garden but nowhere could he find Vappu. At last he flung himself down on a rock to weep.

As he lay there sobbing, all at once the old man with his shining white hair stood beside him and asked:

"Why are you weeping, my boy?"

"I weep because I have lost what is dearer to me than the whole wide world. It is like this: I unlocked the

[101]

twenty-fourth room and there I found the most beautiful of all beautiful maidens. She came with me and we lived together in this castle and all my life was pure joy. Only an hour ago, it seems, we were in this orchard together. I fell asleep, and when I woke up she was gone. Come help me to find her, for I cannot live without her."

"Ha-ha-ho-ho-he-he!" laughed the old man. "Ho-ho-ho-ho! That's the way it always happens when you do what you should have left undone."

"You forget I am a man grown," answered Severi. "Besides, you did not forbid me to enter the twenty-fourth room."

"I told you that you went at your own risk."

"Have it as you will," said Severi. "Only help me to find my Vappu. That is all I ask."

"That's as may be," said the old man. "But tell me, are you wiser now?"

"My sorrow has made me older," Severi answered. "It has made me wiser, too."

Then the old man muttered words of magic under his breath and there stood Vappu before him, radiant as a sunbeam.

"Were you lonesome for me, Severi?" she asked.

"All my happiness went with you," said Severi. "You must promise never to leave me again."

"I promise, but on one condition. I will never leave you again if you can but once hide from me so that I cannot find you. Then, and then only, will I be always with you."

Severi was puzzled. He did not understand what Vappu meant. But the old man whispered in his ear.

"Here is a charm for you. Whenever you wish to hide beyond all seeing, repeat these words, and in the twinkling of an eye you will become invisible. First try hiding in the heart of a fleeing rabbit."

Now the last thing in the world that Severi wanted to do was to hide from Vappu, but he know that if he were to win her he must do as she bade him.

So he ran as fast as his legs could carry him. He ran through fields and meadows, over hills and valleys, and at last he found a rabbit that fled before him through the forest.

"Little Rabbit, Grey Rabbit," Severi called. And the rabbit stood still to listen to his words.

> Thrice I knock at the door of your heart,
> Let me in, Grey Rabbit, let me in.

And the Grey Rabbit opened the door of his heart to Severi, and Severi became invisible and leaped inside.

In the morning when Vappu awoke, she had only to look into her crystal pool. In its clear depths she saw the path that Severi had taken across the meadows and the hills. She saw how he had leapt into the heart of a little grey rabbit. She ran like the wind over the path he had taken, and soon she found him.

"You are not very good at playing hide-and-seek," she laughed, "but you must try again. Perhaps next time you will do better."

This time Severi thought he would enter the heart of a growling bear. He ran until he came to a wild mountain, and there in a deep cave he found a bear. He said:

> Thrice I knock at the door of your heart,
> Let me in, Honeypaw, let me in.

Then he jumped into the warm heart of the bear, and waited.

Next morning Vappu looked again into her crystal

[103]

pool, and saw the path Severi had taken. Once more she ran like the wind until she came to the cave and stood before the growling bear. But when the bear saw Vappu in her beauty he knelt before her, and she cried out laughing:

"Severi, Severi, you cannot hide from me. I have found you, I have found you!"

So Severi came out from his hiding place and walked sadly back with her to the castle.

Again the old man with glistening white hair stood beside Severi.

"Why don't you hide this time within Vappu's own heart?" he asked.

"Thank you for helping me," Severi whispered back, and the next moment he repeated softly:

> Thrice I knock at your door, dear heart,
> Let me in, heart's jewel, let me in!

Then Vappu stared about her in amazement and cried: "Why, Severi was here beside me, and now he is gone!"

She ran to look in her crystal pool but this time it was of no use; she could not see where Severi was hidden.

"*Kultani,* my golden one," cried Severi, "can you not find me?"

"But where are you?" Vappu asked.

"Here in your heart."

"Who led you here?"

"You, Vappu, you led me here."

"And what will you have for your reward?"

"You, Vappu, only you!" cried Severi as he leapt from his hiding place and stood before her.

And from that day forward Severi and Vappu lived in peace in their copper castle, beneath the golden blossoms of the trees and beside the crystal brook.

EI-NIIN-MITA
or
NO-SO-WHAT

There was once a young man named Onni who loved to wander in the deep wild forest. He would take his gun on his shoulder and tramp from morning to night. One day while he was hunting small game, he came to a lake hidden among the trees. He looked across the water, and there he saw three gray ducks. So he hid behind a tree and waited, hoping that they would come near enough for him to shoot them.

All at once a strange thing happened. Onni heard those three ducks talking in his own language.

"Here is a quiet sandy beach," said one.

"It is hidden so well among the fir trees that no one will see us if we change our clothes and go in bathing," said the second.

"Come on," cried the third, flapping its wings and swimming quickly to the shore.

As the three ducks came out from the lake they cast aside their feather robes and turned into three beautiful maidens, who held hands and ran back laughing into the water.

Onni said to himself: "I will steal one of their feathery robes, and see what happens."

So he crept out to the beach, snatched up the robe of the prettiest maiden and carried it back to his hiding place.

When the three maidens had finished bathing they ran to look for their clothes. When they saw that one of their feather robes was missing they were very frightened. Two of them dressed quickly and flew away as gray ducks, but the third maiden ran back and forth along the beach, looking here and there and wringing her hands, and as she ran she repeated this charm:

"You who have stolen my robe, if you are younger than I you shall be my brother: if you are older you shall be my father, and if you are my own age you shall be my husband. Give me back my robe, I pray you."

Onni stepped out, and said:

"Don't be afraid, beautiful maiden, for I mean you no harm. Come with me to my home and I will make you my own true love."

The maiden went back with Onni to his home and became his wife. She was so charming in all her ways that Onni named her Ihana. And as the years went on, she proved such a faithful helpmate that Onni no longer cared to roam the forests as of old. He liked better to stay at home and work in the fields, so that he could be always near her.

It so happened that the news of Ihana's charm and beauty spread far and wide. Everyone envied Onni, for no one had ever seen a woman so lovely and so modest. Her fame reached even the King's castle.

Now the King had a son, who had been searching far and wide for a woman fit to become his bride. But so far every maiden they had seen had some fault or other to be found with her. So the King called his nobles together and said:

"You have sworn that Ihana is the most beautiful woman living?"

"We have sworn," said the nobles.

"Then tell me," said the King, "what is the best way to get rid of this peasant, Onni, so that I may marry her to my son?"

"The best and quickest way," said the oldest noble, nodding his head, "is to send Onni on a long hard journey and ask him to perform some deed that no man can accomplish."

"Tell him that you will cut off his head if he fails," said the second, "and then you will be rid of him forever."

The King called Onni to his castle, and said to him:

"I have heard what a clever man you are, and now you must show me that what they all say of you is true. You must bring me tomorrow a tablecloth upon which are woven the moon and the stars. If you do not bring me the linen before the clock strikes ten, I will have your head cut off."

Onni bowed low, and left the castle with a heavy heart. When he got home he did not tell Ihana what had happened, but she saw his anxious look and knew that he was in trouble.

"What makes you so sad, beloved?" she asked.

"Reason enough to be sad," said Onni. "I shall have my head cut off at ten o'clock tomorrow unless I bring the King a linen tablecloth woven with the moon and the stars."

"Do not worry," Ihana said. "Morning is wiser than nightfall. Go to sleep, and all shall happen as you wish."

As soon as Onni was asleep, Ihana began to weave the linen. Her hands fairly flew. All through the night she toiled, and when morning came the cloth was finished.

Onni thanked her, and proudly took the linen to the King. The King and his nobles examined every inch of it to try and find some fault. But the moon and the stars were so perfectly patterned that they could not find a single flaw in all the work.

So they set about finding a harder task for Onni. After a few days the King sent for him again, and said:

"You have already proved yourself a clever man. Now you must set out on another task. This time you must go to the land of Ei-Niin-Mihin, No-So-Where, and fetch me Ei-Niin-Mita, No-So-What. If you fail in this you lose your head."

Onni trudged home, saying over and over: "Fetch Ei-Niin-Mita from Ei-Niin-Mihin . . . No-So-Where . . . No-So-What . . ."

The longer he walked the sadder he grew, for he had no idea where to begin his search.

"Why are you so sad today?" Ihana asked.

"Good reason, because this time the King will cut off my head for sure. He wants me to go to the land of No-So-Where and fetch him No-So-What. I can never do it, for I don't even know what he means."

"Don't trouble your head, dear Onni," said Ihana.

[108]

"Morning is wiser than nightfall. Go to sleep, and all shall be as you wish."

That night while Onni was sleeping, Ihana set herself to sew. She sewed the night through, and in the morning she gave Onni a handkerchief as delicate as a spider's web and as beautiful as a rainbow.

"Take this magic handkerchief," she said, "and set out on your journey. Make haste, and do not falter nor fear. At nightfall a castle will appear before you. Enter the door and don't be afraid of anything you may see or hear. Hang your wallet, your cap and your mittens on the peg beside the fireplace. Take this handkerchief from your pocket and blow your nose. Be sure that the handkerchief is in plain sight, and make a loud noise about it."

Onni thanked Ihana, kissed her good-bye and set out. The day passed, nightfall came, still he kept on bravely. At last, when the moon and stars began to shine, he saw a strange sight.

Before him was a gaunt gray castle, surrounded by a fence made of human bones. On every fence post but one there grinned a human skull. Onni's knees trembled, but he remembered Ihana's words, and walked bravely in at the open door. In one corner of the great bare room he saw a fat old woman with a hook nose, staring at him.

"*Kas niin* (all right)," said the old woman. "And so! Whenever I am hungry, the fates always send some man to my castle."

Onni was so frightened he wanted to turn and run, but he remembered what Ihana had told him. He acted as if he were quite at home. He hung his wallet, his cap and mittens on a peg by the fireplace. He drew the hand-

[109]

kerchief from his pocket and very loudly blew his nose.

"*Ka,* and so you are my aunt's daughter's husband!" said the old woman at once in a different voice. "What are you doing here? Make yourself at home. What do you want?"

"The King has sent me to the land of No-So-Where to seek No-So-What," Onni replied.

The old woman scratched her head.

" 'Tis a strange hard journey," she said. "Even I do not know where the place is. But wait, I will call my servants."

She hobbled to the door and called into the night: "My servants one and all, come hither!"

There was a whirr of wind and a flutter of wings, and in at the door flew all the birds of the air. There was the wren, the titmouse, the crow and the eagle, and even the loon with his cackling laughter.

"Do you know," shouted the old woman, "what it means to go to the land of No-So-Where and fetch No-So-What?"

"We do not know," chattered all the birds in chorus.

"Then go back to your nests," shouted the old woman.

Again there was a flutter of wings, and then silence.

"I cannot tell you where you will find the land of No-So-Where," said the old woman as she hobbled back to her place in the corner. "But you had best go your way toward the setting sun. My sister lives in a castle like this one of mine. Perhaps she can tell you."

Onni took his wallet, his cap and mittens down from the peg, thanked the old woman and went his way. He walked all night and all the next day. At dusk he came to another gaunt gray castle, fenced about with dead men's bones. He found another grim old woman with a hooked nose. She was twice as large and fat as the first sister.

Again Onni made himself at home. He took the magic handkerchief from his pocket and blew his nose with all his might.

The second sister was surprised. She asked Onni where he was journeying. She called her servants, but could not learn the way to the land of No-So-Where, so she sent Onni on to the castle of the third sister.

Onni continued his journey until he saw a third gaunt gray castle. Here he found a third old woman three times as large and three times as grim as the first sister.

The third old woman saw the magic handkerchief, and asked Onni where he was journeying.

"I am on my way to the land of No-So-Where, to fetch No-So-What."

The old woman shook her head, hobbled to the door and called into the night: "Arise, my servants all, and come hither!"

There was a loud croaking and a thumping outside, and big toads and small toads began hopping into the room through the doorway.

"Tell me how to find the land of No-So-Where," the old woman shouted.

"We don't know what you are talking about," the toads replied in a deep chorus.

"Are you all gathered here?" called the old woman.

"Our eldest brother is still on his way," answered the toads in chorus. "He may be able to tell."

"Good," said the old woman. "The rest of you return to the marshes."

There was a croaking and a thumping, then silence.

Soon, however, a great wrinkled toad hopped into the

[111]

middle of the room. He looked a thousand years old.

"I know the place where No-So-What lies hidden in the land of No-So-Where," said the toad.

"Good," said the old woman. She filled Onni's wallet with bread and meat and wine. "Follow this toad wherever he goes. Fear nothing, and he will bring you safely to the end of your journey."

The toad hopped briskly out of the room, across the garden, and into the path that led through the deep dark woods. Onni followed. All night long they journeyed, and at nightfall the next day they came to a great gray castle like the one they had left.

The toad hopped onto the doorstep, the door opened, and the toad plopped himself down in the middle of the great bare room and looked about him. Again Onni followed.

There was a shelf on the wall beside the great fireplace. The toad hopped up on this, and Onni followed. Behind the shelf was an opening, and into this the toad leapt. Onni followed, and by standing on tiptoe could just see over the shelf.

After a long time the door opened, and a hunter entered with a great bag of game slung across his shoulder. He threw the bag on the floor, looked about the room to make sure he was alone, and said softly:

"No-So-What."

"What?" answered a tiny voice from within the very wall where Onni was hiding.

"Bring me food. Hurry! I'm hungry!" continued the hunter.

There appeared as by magic a table set with every kind of food. The hunter ate his fill, and then said:

"No-So-What, clear the food away."

[112]

The table and the food disappeared. The hunter got up from his chair, yawned and stretched himself, and went into another room to sleep.

"This must be No-So-Where," thought Onni to himself, "and this must be No-So-What. But how can I take it back to the King?"

The toad hopped out from behind the wall into the middle of the floor, and Onni followed.

"No-So-What," whispered Onni.

"What?" answered the tiny voice.

"Bring me food," said Onni.

The table appeared as by magic and Onni ate his fill.

"No-So-What," called Onni.

"What?"

"Clear the food away."

The table disappeared.

"I wonder if No-So-What will follow me," thought Onni to himself.

"No-So-What," he called.

"What?"

"I'm going on a journey. Will you come with me?"

"I will come with you," answered the tiny voice.

The toad hopped out of the castle, across the garden.

"I am in the garden. No-So-What, are you coming?" called Onni.

"Here I am," answered the tiny voice. "I'm going along the path through the deep woods."

Onni followed the toad and the voice followed Onni. After many hours, Onni called:

"No-So-What."

"Here I am."

"I am hungry," said Onni. "Bring food."

The table appeared as by magic, and Onni again ate.

[113]

"Clear away the food, and follow me," said Onni.

The table and the food vanished, and Onni walked again behind the toad.

At last the toad led Onni back to the castle of the third sister. Onni thanked the Old Woman and the toad, and went his way alone with the voice.

At the end of another day Onni came to the shore of the sea. A ship was just lifting anchor and setting out for Onni's native land, so he climbed aboard.

"No-So-What," called Onni in a voice so low that no one else would hear, "I am stepping into the ship."

"Here I am," said the tiny voice.

The next day Onni was hungry. When no one was listening he called:

"No-So-What, I'm almost starved. Bring food enough for me and for all the sailors."

A great table appeared laden with every kind of food, and Onni and the sailors ate and drank their fill. The sailors were so pleased that they wanted to trade with Onni for his magic table.

"I have a marvelous anvil," said the Captain. "See, it is so small I can carry it in my pocket. But when I hit it three blows with this golden hammer, out come twelve soldiers with armor and swords to fight for me. I will trade you my magic anvil for your magic table."

"It is a bargain," said Onni.

The Captain gave him the anvil and the hammer, and Onni hid them in the bottom of his pocket.

After many days the ship came to anchor in Onni's native land. Onni left the magic table laden with wonderful food, and went ashore. As he was leaving he said:

"No-So-What."

"Here I am," said the tiny voice.

[114]

"I am going to the King's castle. Follow me."

When Onni reached the castle, he learned that the King had called all his people together to celebrate the wedding of the Prince and Ihana.

The Prince sat at the head of the table, smiling, for was he not going to marry Ihana, the most beautiful woman in the kingdom? But at the foot of the table sat Ihana herself, very sad, for she had been told that Onni had died before reaching the end of his long journey.

Onni took the magic handkerchief from his pocket, and loudly blew his nose. When Ihana saw Onni, she rushed from the table, threw her arms about his neck and cried:

"Wicked King, I will never marry your son, even if you kill me. This is Onni, my beloved."

The King was so angry that he ordered his soldiers to take Onni and cut off his head.

Onni thought of his magic anvil, and struck it three blows with the golden hammer. Twelve giant soldiers, all in armor, with drawn swords, appeared by magic. They drove the King and his nobles from the castle.

So now Onni and his Ihana were King and Queen, and the people greeted them gladly. And the first thing Onni did was to call:

"Ei-Niin-Mita, No-So-What."

"Here I am," came the tiny voice.

"Bring me food for me and my people!"

Great tables appeared, loaded with food and drink, and all the people gathered round and feasted as they had never feasted before. For three days and three nights the feasting lasted. When it was over Onni and Ihana went back to their castle, and there was happiness throughout their kingdom for ever after.

THE GIRL WHO SOUGHT HER NINE
BROTHERS

Once upon a time there was an old man and an old
woman who had nine sons, but no daughters. One day
when the boys were doing their tasks about the house,
they began to wish they had a sister. So they sent the
eldest brother to his mother.

"When the fairies next bring you a child," he said,
"ask for a girl."

The mother only smiled, and the eldest son and all
of his brothers grew angry, for they thought their
mother did not wish to please them. The eldest brother
went back to his mother a second time and said: "My
brothers and I have decided to leave home, and unless
you ask for a sister for us, we shall never come back to
live with you again."

There was a troubled look on the mother's face this time, but she made no promise. The eldest brother continued:

"I'll tell you what we have decided to do, Mother. When the next child is brought you, if it is a girl, set a spindle outside the door. If it is a boy, set an axe. One of us will return to look for the sign. If it is a girl, we will all return and care for you in your old age; but if it is another boy, you will never see us again."

After a few weeks the fairies brought another baby, and this time it was a girl. The mother was very happy as she set the spindle outside the door.

In the night, however, an ogress came, and changed the spindle into an axe handle. The eldest brother returned, and when he saw the sign, he went back to his brothers and told them that the sign meant the fairies had brought another boy.

From that day on, nothing was heard or seen of the boys. The baby daughter was named Vieno, and she lived with her parents just as though she had been an only child.

When Vieno reached womanhood, her mother told her about her nine lost brothers. She also told of finding an axe handle where she had put a spindle, which made her sure that she and her sons had been tricked by a cruel ogress.

After Vieno had heard all that had happened, she began to weep. For she was sorry for her lonely mother, and she was sad because she had no brothers. Her mother tried to comfort her, but she only wept the more.

At last her mother began to collect Vieno's tears in an earthen jar, and when it was full, she mixed the tears with flour and made a great round loaf of bread.

[117]

She moulded a hole in the center of the loaf. Then she said to Vieno:

"Dry your tears, my daughter. Find a faithful companion who will set forth with you into the wide world to seek your brothers."

It so happened that Vieno had a small spotted dog that she loved dearly.

"Mother, let me go alone to seek my brothers! I have my dog Pilkka. He is faithful. He is all the companion I shall need!"

When the mother at last consented, Vieno took Pilkka and the loaf her mother had made from her own tears, and started forth on her long journey. But first she set the round loaf of bread before her in the road, and sang a charm to it:

> Viere, viere, kakkarani,
> Yhdeksän veikkosihin
> Yksihin emon eloihin.

> Roll, roll, round bread, roll,
> Bring me my brothers nine
> Men of mother's and mine.

The charm worked, and the loaf of bread began to roll. Vieno and Pilkka followed it down the long road. They had not journeyed far when they met an ogress, the very ogress who had charmed the spindle into an axe handle when Vieno was born. The ogress spoke to Vieno:

"May I have the pleasure of walking with you, my girl?"

Although Vieno did not know the old woman, she was frightened, and Pilkka growled. But the ogress walked on beside Vieno, behind the rolling loaf. Together they trudged the weary miles. When Vieno's feet were like lead, she and the ogress came to a sparkling pool.

"It will rest us to bathe our tired feet," said the ogress. "You look worn and weary."

Vieno was ready to bathe her feet, but Pilkka growled:

"Do not go near the water, Mistress Vieno, for if you do the ogress will put her charm upon you."

Vieno understood what Pilkka said, and answered the ogress:

"You are quite mistaken. I am not tired, and would rather to go on with my journey. But you may rest beside the pool if you like."

The ogress was very angry with Pilkka, and kicked him so hard that she broke one of his hind legs. Vieno was sorry, and wanted to cry, but all that she could do was to repeat her charm:

> Roll, roll, round bread, roll,
> Bring me my brothers nine
> Men of mother's and mine.

The loaf of bread again rolled before them. Vieno and the ogress walked side by side, while poor Pilkka limped painfully behind. After many weary hours had passed, the ogress, Vieno, and Pilkka came to another sparkling pool.

"You must be very weary, my maiden," said the ogress. "Let us now bathe and refresh ourselves."

Pilkka growled:

"Don't go into the water, my Vieno, or the ogress will surely work magic on you."

Vieno obeyed the dog's warning, and the ogress was twice as angry as before. Again she kicked poor Pilkka, breaking one of his front legs.

[119]

"This will put an end to you, you *Paholainen* (Wicked one) ," she said to herself.

Vieno wiped the tears from her eyes, but once more all she could do was to look straight ahead, repeating the charm:

> Roll, roll, round bread, roll,
> Bring me my brothers nine
> Men of mother's and mine.

Poor Pilkka still hopped along on his two legs, calling in a plaintive tone:

"Even if I die, my Mistress, do not bathe in any pool with the ogress, for she will surely put you under a charm."

Again they came to a cool pool, and the ogress said:

"My feet are sore and blistered. You too must be very tired, my maiden. Come, let us rest for a few minutes. Then we will bathe."

But Vieno remembered Pilkka's words, and still trudged after the rolling loaf of bread. The ogress was now three times as angry as before, and in her rage she spoke a charm that destroyed poor Pilkka at once. He vanished into a cloud of dust.

"Now we shall see," the ogress muttered to herself.

By the time they reached the next pool, Vieno was so very hot and tired that she forgot everything, even Pilkka's warning.

"It can do us no harm to rest in the water for a few minutes," crooned the ogress.

And this time Vieno agreed.

"You splash my face and I will splash yours," said the ogress.

Vieno did not like to do this, but the ogress coaxed her, and so Vieno made a cup of her hand, and began

She would chant a song

splashing the water, while the ogress splashed back at her. After a while, the ogress repeated the charm:

"Your body to me, mine to you."

Instantly the ogress became young and beautiful, and Vieno became old and brown and ugly. Then the ogress put a spell on Vieno so that she could not use her tongue to tell anyone what had happened.

Once again the ogress and Vieno started on their way, but this time the ogress repeated the charm:

> Roll, roll, round bread, roll
> Bring me my brothers nine,
> Men of mother's and mine.

It was not long afterward that the round tear-bread loaf led them through a gate, and into a garden beside a house in which Vieno's nine brothers lived. The ogress snatched the round loaf in her arms, and held it before her.

The brothers came into the garden and asked:

"Who are you, and from what far country have you come?"

Poor Vieno, who was now old and ugly, moved her lips, but no sound came from them. The young and beautiful ogress answered:

"Greetings, my nine brothers. You have never seen me, but I am your sister."

"But why was the axe handle placed beside the door?" asked the eldest brother.

"Mother placed a spindle beside the door, but a spiteful ogress came in the night, and changed the spindle into an axe handle," the ogress continued. "When I grew to womanhood, my mother told me how the trick had driven you all away. I begged my mother to let

[122]

me search for you. I was so lonely that I wept my tears into an earthen jar, and mother took the tear-water and made this bread. This round loaf rolled along the road before me, and showed me the way to your door."

The brothers believed the ogress, took her into their house, and treated her kindly in every way as a young sister should be treated.

"But why did you bring this ugly old woman with you?" the eldest brother asked as he pointed at Vieno.

"I thought she might be useful to herd your cattle in the fields," said the ogress.

This satisfied the brothers, so that they questioned her no more.

Soon the ogress became head of their house, and had everything she could possibly wish. But poor Vieno worked alone in the fields early and late, in the wind and the rain and the heat of the noonday sun.

Early every morning, the ogress led Vieno down to the river where she gave her back her tongue for the day so that she could call the cattle. But every evening before Vieno came back to the house, she charmed her so that she could not speak.

The ogress treated her spitefully in every way, putting burrs in her shoes, and stones in her bread. While Vieno would watch the cattle, she would chant a song that she had made up herself, telling aloud the story of her sorrows. Thus time went on, and Vieno was more sorrowful than she had ever been.

One day it chanced that the youngest brother was chopping wood close by the edge of the meadow. The wind was warm and gentle, and carried the plaintive voice of Vieno to his ear. At first he thought the cow-woman was talking to the cattle. But after he had heard

[123]

snatches of her song, he called his brothers to see what it all might mean. They stood and listened.

> Kule, päivä, kuusikolle,
> Viere, kuusi, koivikolle

> Fly, bright day! Fly, bright day!
> Fly into the fir forest
> Glide into the birch glade
> March over the meadows
> Carry the cattle-girl
> Harmless to her home.
> Fly, bright day! Fly, bright day!
> The Ogress oppresses me
> Bakes stones in my bread,
> Dulls my knife upon a stone
> Makes me mean and speechless.

> Fly, bright day! Fly, bright day!
> Roll, roll, tear-bread, roll,
> Bring me my brothers nine,
> Men of mother's and mine.

The brothers called the cow-woman to them and said to her:

"How is it you sing to yourself in the meadows, but in the house you say nothing?"

"I am your rightful sister," answered Vieno. "The woman you keep in your house is a spiteful ogress. Years ago she changed the spindle our mother set beside the door into an axe handle to deceive you. When I was following the tear-bread on my way to find you, this same ogress took my body and gave me hers. Only when I come here to watch the cattle does she give me my tongue. In the evening she meets me by the river and charms me so that I cannot tell you the truth."

When the brothers heard this they were very angry.

"We will revenge ourselves on the wicked ogress,"

they said, "but first we must remove the charm from you, our rightful sister, and give your beautiful body back to you. Tomorrow at noonday, leave the cattle in the meadow. Keep your eyes covered with your hands, and when you reach the house, say to the ogress that your eyes hurt so you cannot see in the sun. We will be there, and together we will turn aside the charm."

Vieno did as she was bid. On the morrow she came into the house when the ogress was busy putting the food on the table, and least expected her.

"Why do you come in from the meadows at midday?" the ogress growled.

"I cannot stand the light of the sun," answered Vieno.

The brothers were waiting, and now they came into the house to sit down at the table. They too asked why the cow-woman had left the meadows at noonday.

"My eyes pain me," said Vieno.

"Dash water in her eyes, and send her away," the eldest brother said to the ogress.

The ogress waited till she thought Vieno was not watching, then quickly threw the water into her face. But Vieno was on her guard, and said swiftly:

"My own body to me, yours to you."

The charm worked, Vieno became again her own beautiful self, while the ogress grew old and brown and ugly.

The brothers leapt up from the table and rushed at the ogress to seize her, but the ogress ran through the doorway and fled. The eldest brother shouted after her:

"If ever you come near us again, we'll destroy you!"

Thereupon Vieno and her brothers returned to their home, and told their father and mother all that had happened. And together they lived happily ever after.

[125]

THE TWO PINE CONES

A Laplander wizard was once journeying through Finland. At nightfall he came to a town where he wished to spend the night. But as he had no money he had to beg for a lodging.

The first house he passed was a tiny hut built of logs, on the edge of the town. It was so small that the wizard passed it by, thinking he might go to a larger house where the folk would be better able to lodge him.

The next house was quite big: one could see it belonged to well-to-do folk. So he knocked at the door. At first there was no answer, then a gruff voice called out:

"Who comes knocking on decent folk's doors at this hour?"

The wizard answered softly: "A wayfarer, who begs a corner by your stove for the night."

The woman answered:

"You can go elsewhere, then. I've no room for beggars. Move on, or I'll set the dogs after you."

The wizard went back to the poor hut at the edge of the town. He knocked, and a kindly looking woman opened the door. She and her husband at once asked him in, sat him down at their table with them to eat, and when bed-time came they gave him their only bed.

In the morning, to pay for his lodging, the wizard wished to give the woman the ring he wore on his finger, as he had no money. But she refused it. So instead he gave her a pine cone which would bring good luck to the first work she undertook that day.

The woman took the pine cone and thanked him. Then she turned to her work. Her first job that morning was to measure the linen she had woven the day before. She measured and measured, and to her surprise there was so much linen that it took her three whole days to measure it all. And by that time there was enough linen to last her family for the rest of their lives.

The story of the poor woman's good fortune was told up and down the village. It soon reached the ears of her rich neighbor who had turned the wizard away. She was sorry enough now, and made up her mind she would have a different answer for the Laplander if he ever came her way again.

A year passed. Again the wizard passed through the town. Once more he went to the big house to ask for a night's lodging, but this time the woman received him smiling, offering him the best of food in the house and the finest feather bed to sleep on.

In the morning the wizard wished to pay her for her kindness, but she refused his money. Then he gave her a pine cone, as he had done to the poor woman, saying:

"This will bring you luck to the first job you undertake."

Now the greedy woman had been waiting for this very gift, and had set out a purse of gold on her table, all ready to count her money. But in her excitement she sneezed before she reached the table, and without thinking she ran to get a handkerchief. And for three whole days she could do nothing but sneeze, run for her handkerchief, and sneeze again. Not till the three days were over could she stop sneezing even long enough to put away the purse of gold!

KALLE AND THE WOOD GROUSE

Kalle was said to be the greatest hunter in his native village. Even when all his neighbors came home empty-handed from the deep wild forest, Kalle always managed to bring back a rabbit or a wild duck. He lived in a little hut with his wife and poor though they were, they were as happy as birds.

But one day when Kalle went out hunting with his dog, he had no luck at all. From early morning he had tramped without seeing so much as the track of a squirrel. At last as evening gathered down, he turned his skiis toward home. All at once his dog came upon a wood grouse perched high in a fir tree. The dog began to bark.

Kalle stopped short, drew his bow and let fly an arrow, but missed. As he was drawing a second arrow the grouse cried out:

"Please do not kill me. I am as fond of life as you are."

Kalle was very surprised to hear the bird speaking in a language he could understand. All the same he thought he would be a fool not to shoot, so again he drew his bow. And again, before he could shoot, the bird called out:

"If you kill me, I'll bring you bad luck as long as you live."

"You will, will you," thought Kalle, and a third time he took aim.

"If you take me home and feed me for a year," the grouse called down, "I'll reward you well for your trouble."

Kalle had quite enough to do feeding his wife and himself, but still these words set him thinking. In the end he slung his bow across his shoulder again and told the grouse to follow him home.

"This bird has promised to reward me if I will feed him for a year," he told his wife. "What do you think about it?"

"*Ka,* feed him by all means," said his wife. "He won't eat much and maybe he'll bring us luck after all. Stranger things have happened before now."

So Kalle fed the grouse faithfully each day, and after several months he noticed a copper quill beginning to grow on one of its tail feathers. At the end of the year the grouse one day dropped the copper quill from its tail and flew away.

Kalle's wife laughed.

"So there's your reward for keeping the grouse! All you get for your pains is a tail feather!"

At nightfall the grouse returned and pleaded:

"Do not kill me, Kalle, for I prize my life. Feed me

for just another year and you shall have your reward."

At the end of the second year Kalle had a silver quill this time for his trouble, and again his wife laughed. She said: "Your grouse is pretty poor pay!"

Again the bird returned, and said:

"Kalle, feed me a third year, and you shall never be sorry."

This time the grouse dropped a golden quill from his tail. And while Kalle's wife was still laughing about it, the grouse said to Kalle:

"You have been kind to me for three years. Now you shall have your reward. Climb on my back, and we will go in search of the Chest Without a Key."

As the grouse spoke, he suddenly began to grow larger and larger, till he was bigger than any bird that man had ever dreamed. When Kalle's wife saw the spread of his great wings, she cried out in terror.

"Kalle, you must not go on this wild journey! What do we want with a chest without a key!"

But Kalle only laughed.

"Don't be afraid," he said. "The bird has done us no harm so far. And besides, I shall soon be back again."

As he spoke, he climbed on the bird's back. The bird spread his great wings and carried him high into the sky, out across the sea. As he flapped upward he asked:

"How does the sea look to you now, Kalle?"

"It is like the deep bottom of a sieve," Kalle answered.

Without warning the great bird turned on his side, and Kalle slid from his back and began falling through the air. Just before Kalle struck the water, the grouse swooped down, caught him on his back again, and said:

"Now you know the terror I felt when you first shot an arrow at me."

[131]

As the grouse flew still higher into the heavens, he asked presently:

"How does the sea look to you now?"

"No larger than a golden ring," Kalle answered.

Again the bird dropped Kalle, and a second time swooped down and caught him on his back.

"Now you know how I felt the second time you aimed at me."

A third time the bird flew skyward, but much higher.

"How does the sea look to you now, Kalle?" it asked.

"No larger than the eye of a needle."

A third time Kalle felt himself falling through space. But just as he neared the water, the great bird caught him as before.

"So I felt," the grouse said, "the third time you were about to shoot at me. Each time my fear became greater."

"But please do not drop me again," Kalle pleaded. "I have suffered enough."

"I will not," answered the grouse. "I will have pity on you as you had pity on me."

Now they were flying far out across the land. As the bird flapped his great wings he asked:

"Do you see anything ahead?"

"Far away," said Kalle, "I seem to see a copper tower."

"That is where my youngest sister dwells," said the grouse. "When we reach her castle I will tell her how you befriended me. She will want to reward you. Ask her then for the Chest Without a Key."

Soon they came to the copper castle. As they touched the ground, the bird changed into a man, and led Kalle through the arched doorway. The youngest sister asked:

"*Ka,* my brother, where have you been these three years?"

He answered: "This man, Kalle, fed me and gave me shelter."

The sister asked Kalle:

"What can I give you for a reward?"

"I should like," answered Kalle, "the Chest Without a Key."

"I am sorry," said the sister. "I have not got it. You may have anything else. I can give you silver, gold, jewels, but not the Chest Without a Key."

Once more the brother changed himself into a great bird, took Kalle on his back and flew until it seemed to Kalle they must have reached the end of the world.

Presently the bird asked: "Do you see anything ahead?"

"I see a great silver tower," Kalle said.

"That is the home of my second sister," said the bird. "Ask her for the Chest Without a Key."

But the second sister said: "I am sorry. I have not got the Chest Without a Key. Ask me anything else you will."

A third time the great bird flew with Kalle for what seemed to him many days. At last the bird said:

"See the great golden castle ahead. This is where my eldest sister dwells. Now at last you will have the Chest Without a Key."

The eldest sister greeted her brother, heard how kind Kalle had been, and gladly gave him the Chest.

This time, as before, the brother changed into a great bird, took Kalle and his Chest upon its back, and after a long flight set him down at the foot of a lonely mountain.

Then the grouse spoke to Kalle for the last time:

"Your courage and your kindness have broken the

[133]

charm that the great magician, Crooked Circle, placed upon me. Many long years ago, Crooked Circle became angry with my father, who was a great king. Out of spite he changed me into a grouse, and only once each day could I become a man. The spell could only be broken, the magician said, if some man should take me home, give me food and shelter for three long years, then dare to ride upon my back to the far Northland. You, Kalle, my friend, have broken the spell. And as a reward, the magic Chest Without a Key is yours."

When he had finished speaking, the bird flew away, leaving Kalle alone.

Kalle sat down. He waited and waited for the bird to return, but it did not come. Night passed, and when morning came he took the Chest upon his shoulder and started to walk. He had no idea in which direction his home lay. He stumbled on, and as he went the Chest grew heavier and heavier. At last he was so tired that he flung it on the ground.

As the Chest touched the ground it flew open, and all at once Kalle found himself in the hall of a great castle, seated at a table covered with meat and drink. Servants stood by, ready to serve him.

"This is a fine castle," Kalle said to himself. "I am master here. There is food and drink, and there are beds to sleep on. I can live here in comfort all my days."

But before long he grew restless. He thought of his wife, and of their hut in the forest. He wanted to leave his fine castle and set out once more to find his home.

As he started on his way, he met a stranger who said:

"Kalle, if you will give me what has been born at your home while you were away, I will lead you back to your wife."

Kalle thought it over and said to himself: "Perhaps there are kittens or puppies, or maybe the old speckled hen has hatched out a brood of chickens by this time." So he replied:

"It is a bargain. Lead me back to my wife, and you shall have whatever has been born during my journey."

"Then follow me," said the man. "But what about the Chest? Are you going to leave it behind?"

Kalle looked about him, and saw with surprise that the fine castle had vanished. But the Chest, tightly closed as before, lay on the rocks, and he hoisted it to his shoulder.

Then there came a strange clicking in Kalle's ears and the next thing he knew there stood his own cottage before him. Here he saw his wife running out with a bundle in her arms. She called:

"See, Kalle, see! This is Jaakko. He was born while you were away."

Then Kalle wept and cried, for he knew he had given away his only son. Calling the stranger aside, he begged him to leave Jaakko with his mother until the child had grown to manhood.

The man agreed to this, but said to Kalle:

"*Ka,* I am Väärä-Pyörä, the Magician, Crooked Circle. The boy may stay here with you till he is grown, but when I call him you must let him go, or a curse will fall upon your household. Bury the Chest Without a Key in the ground behind your hut, where no man will find it. Leave it there until a man asks you to dig it up. Then you shall have your reward."

As soon as he had finished speaking, Crooked Circle disappeared.

Years passed, and Jaakko grew mightily. Each year he

[135]

became stronger and stronger, so that when he wrestled with boys his own age, he always hurt them. He was so strong he could catch a wild bull by its horns, twisting its neck, and holding it still.

The young men of the village complained because Jaakko was rough. They pointed their fingers at him and grumbled:

"You food of Crooked Circle, why do you always cripple your friends?"

Jaakko did not know what they meant. So he went to his mother and asked:

"Why do they call me food of Crooked Circle?"

His mother did not know, and called Kalle to solve the riddle. Then, for the first time, Kalle told her his story:

"I was lost far from home. I made a bargain with an unknown man, who later told me his name was Crooked Circle. He promised to guide me home, if in return I would give him whatever had been born at home while I way away. I never thought I was giving away my only son."

When Jaakko heard this story, he was eager to find Crooked Circle at once, and demand his release. And he was so strong that his parents could not hold him back.

So Jaakko mounted his horse and set out. He rode fast, and when his horse was tired, he turned it loose and ran on alone. After many days he came to the seashore.

Here on the sands, Jaakko met the most beautiful girl he had ever seen, and at once fell in love with her.

"You must be my wife," he told her.

The maiden answered:

[136]

"Come with me to my palace under the sea"

The island where the birds sing day and night

A hunter happened to pass that way

The black lamb, Musti, strayed into the woods

Eight men held each bag open to the sunlight

"What are you staring up here for?"

"That's as may be, but first you must see my father."

"Who are you?" Jaakko asked.

"I am Impi, the only daughter of Crooked Circle."

"It is Crooked Circle I am seeking," said Jaakko with a strange light in his eyes. "Show me where he lives."

Impi took Jaakko by the hand, leading him far along the yellow sands. At last she stopped and said:

"See the high turret beyond yonder rock? There you will find Crooked Circle. But before you reach the castle door, you will see a heavy iron bar thrust into the ground. You must pull the bar from the ground before you knock at the door. Hang this charm about your neck, for it will make you invisible so that my father and his soldiers cannot see you. . . . Now I will run on ahead. Try your strength, and as soon as you have pulled the iron bar from the ground, come to me in my room in the castle, and I will be your bride. May success be yours."

The maiden let go of Jaakko's hand, ran lightly along the yellow sands and over the rocks, and disappeared.

Jaakko hurried forward. When he found the iron bar, he saw that the ground about it had been trampled hard as stone by the feet of other youths who had striven there, without being able to move it.

But Jaakko did not lose courage. He seized the bar with both his hands, and pulled with all his might. And he was so strong that the bar leapt from the ground, flying against the castle wall with such force that it shook the very turrets.

It so happened that just then Crooked Circle was seated at his dinner in the great hall. When he heard the noise, and felt the castle tremble, he said to his highest general:

"We are going to have guests. They must be very

powerful men since they shake the castle with their coming. Go to the door and tell me who they are."

The General returned after a minute, and said:

"The iron bar is surely jerked from the ground, but I can see no guests coming."

"This is strange," said Crooked Circle. "I do not understand it."

Jaakko, with the charm of invisibility about his neck, hurried through the castle, and into Impi's room.

"According to custom," said Impi, "you must first speak to my father before you can claim me as your bride."

Jaakko removed the charm from his breast, went to Crooked Circle, and said:

"When I was a mere child, my father, Kalle, gave me to you by mistake. Now that I am a man, I have come to ask you for your daughter, Impi. I desire her for my wife."

"You are surely in a great hurry," replied Crooked Circle, surprised at the young man's courage. "There will be time to talk about Impi later. You must first build me a castle that will reach from the ground to the skies. When that is finished you must, in one single night, sow wheat, plow, raise, reap, and grind it, and then bake me bread from the flour. And when this is done, you must bring me three wood grouse with iron beaks from behind the nine seas."

As Jaakko heard the words of Crooked Circle, his face grew white and his hands trembled.

"But you do not understand," he said: "I am no magician."

Crooked Circle laughed till the walls of the castle shook, "I thought as much," he replied. "But you can learn. For a hundred years you shall be my servant. In that time I can teach you many strange things."

When Crooked Circle had finished, Jaakko returned to Impi, and told her all that her father had said.

"A hundred years!" laughed Impi, clapping her hands. "This time we shall outwit the master magician. In the stable are nine wonderful horses. We will charm seven of them, so that they can only walk. On the other two we can escape."

Jaakko and Impi used the charm to make themselves invisible, and made their way to the stable. There they charmed the seven horses, as they had planned, and galloped away unseen.

When Crooked Circle found that they were gone, he had to run after them on foot. As Impi saw him coming, she leapt from her horse, drew a magic *huivi* (head shawl) from her breast, and struck the ground three times.

Instantly there arose a mountain so high that Crooked Circle was forced to return to the castle and look into his magic globe to see which way they had gone.

When Crooked Circle was about to overtake them a second time, Impi worked a second charm. She turned one of the horses into a chapel and the other into a bell tower. She herself became a robed minister and Jaakko a simple sexton.

Crooked Circle came bounding into the bell tower, and found Jaakko ringing the bell, but did not know him. He asked breathlessly:

"Have you seen two travellers on horseback pass this way?"

"Yes, a man and a woman came this way," answered Jaakko. "They turned to the left on the road yonder."

Off hurried Crooked Circle, and Impi and Jaakko rode on, laughing.

Crooked Circle searched a long time, then again hastened back to his magic globe to learn which way they had gone. This time, when they saw him coming, Impi caused a magic river to flow behind them, so wide and so deep that Crooked Circle could not cross it.

Crooked Circle saw now that his daughter was far too clever for him, so he returned to his castle and gave up the chase in despair.

When they saw that they were no longer in danger, Jaakko led Impi back to his home. Kalle and his wife wept with joy to see their son standing once more before them, safe and sound, his beautiful bride at his side. And after Jaakko had told them all the long story of his adventures, he said:

"Now it is time for us to dig up the Chest Without a Key."

They found the heavy chest where it had lain for so many years, buried in the ground behind the hut, and when they brought it into the house Impi showed them a key which exactly fitted the lock. They opened the chest, and there poured forth from it a stream of gold and jewels, enough to last them all in riches to the end of their days.

And so it was, after waiting all those many long years, that Kalle had his reward from the wood grouse at last.

NIILO AND THE WIZARD

Once upon a time there was a poor farmer named Tauno, who lived happily in his *tupa* with his wife, and his only son, Niilo. He worked in his garden, tending his cattle, and hoping to get money to send Niilo to school. But everything seemed to go wrong. One year the frost killed his fruit. The next year blight destroyed his corn. So it went, and in spite of all his planning, he remained poor.

One evening a wizard came to Tauno's door, asking if he might have a bed for the night. The farmer invited him to come in and make himself at home.

During the evening the wizard noticed Niilo, and saw what a bright lad he was. To amuse the boy, the wizard began to do tricks of magic. He took a live rabbit out of Niilo's pocket, where a moment before there had been only a few shiny pebbles and a little ball of birch bark. And from Niilo's cap he drew a bright shawl, which he gave to Niilo's mother.

Niilo's eyes sparkled. He laughed with joy, and wished that he, too, could do wonderful tricks like these.

The wizard saw that he would make an apt pupil, and in the morning begged Tauno to let him take Niilo with him on his travels.

"I will teach the boy all my wisdom," said the wizard. "It will cost you never a penny."

Tauno and his wife thought this a good offer, and so Niilo became the magician's pupil. With him he travelled to the far Pohjola (the North Country), to Lapland, where old women taught him how to cure fevers and to ward off evil. He learned the most secret magic charms, so that he could change himself into any bird or beast at will.

Some years later, when the wizard had taught Niilo all his art, he returned to Tauno and demanded that the poor farmer pay him a thousand rubles.

"It has cost me a lot of money to keep Niilo all these years," he said, "and besides, the magic I have taught him is worth many times that price."

"But have you forgotten our agreement?" asked Tauno. "You said it would not cost me a penny!"

While they were still arguing Niilo drew his father aside.

"I have a plan," he said. "If you'll help me, we'll get a thousand roubles from the wizard instead of you paying him, and have plenty over for ourselves besides."

"I'll gladly help you," said the father, who was nearly in despair. "But I don't see how you'll get the wizard to pay instead of us."

"Don't worry about that," said Niilo. "I know a trick or two myself. I haven't lived with the wizard and the old Lapland women for nothing."

[142]

He explained his plan, and when he had done he went into the stable and changed himself by magic into a beautiful white horse. Then the father led the horse out, and traded it to the wizard for the thousand roubles.

The wizard took the horse off to market to sell it. On the way he stopped at an inn to eat his dinner, leaving the horse hitched to a post outside.

While no one was watching, Niilo changed back into his real self, returned to his father, and said:

"Now that we have paid the debt, we'll get some money from the wizard for ourselves. I will change myself this time into a beautiful bay horse, and you will take me to the market and sell me to the wizard for two thousand roubles. There is only one thing you must remember. When you sell me, do not leave the bridle and reins upon me, for if you do, I won't be able to change myself back into a man."

Tauno did as he was bid, but this time the wizard, suspecting trickery, would not let him remove the bridle and reins. The result was that Tauno went home with more money than he had ever had in his life, but poor Niilo had to remain tied in the wizard's stable.

When winter came, the wizard set out to market to sell the horse at a profit. The way was long, and he stopped at an inn for dinner.

It happened that a crowd of mischievous boys passed down the street where the horse was tied, whereupon he begged the boys to loosen the reins and set him free. They did this, and Niilo was at last ready to change himself back into a man.

But at the very instant the boys freed him, the wizard finished his dinner, and came out into the street. And Niilo had to run for his life.

[143]

He set off at a gallop towards a frozen lake, with the wizard close at his heels. Niilo sped across the ice until he came to a great air hole. He jumped through the hole into the water, and changed himself into a small perch.

The wizard, not to be outdone, jumped through the ice, too, changed himself into a large pike, and began chasing the tiny perch in order to eat him.

Then Niilo turned himself into a small gold ring, and sank to the sandy bottom of the lake. There the wizard could not find him.

It so happened that the waves washed the golden ring up on the shore near a King's castle. When spring came the ladies of the Court, who were strolling along the beach, found the ring and carried it to the King's daughter. The Princess was very pleased, and placed it on her finger.

Niilo was happy, too, for he thought the Princess very beautiful, and he wished he might one day claim her for his wife. At last one morning as the Princess was bathing her hands in perfumed water, Niilo slid from her finger into the bowl. From the bowl of water he bounced to the floor, spun around the Princess three times, then rolled into a corner, where he lay hidden.

The Princess at once began to cry, for she thought she had lost her lovely golden ring. She did not know that Niilo had charmed her by spinning about her three times, and that she would fall in love with him the first moment she saw him in his true form.

As she wept, she was startled by a deep, strong voice. It came from the corner of the room. Then she saw her ring lying there. No sooner had she noticed the ring than it changed by magic into a handsome young man.

[144]

Niilo knelt before the Princess and said:

"Lovely Princess, I am a man changed into a ring. I am under the spell of an evil wizard. He is now chasing me, and I shall soon be forced to change myself back into a ring, so that I may escape him. Tomorrow he will come to the castle, and offer the King, your father, a fabulous price for me. But do not allow the King to sell me. If he insists, drop me to the floor.

"I shall then change myself into a hundred green peas. The wizard, not to be outwitted, will then disguise himself as a rooster, and begin to peck at the peas. But before he knows what is happening, I shall turn into a fox and gobble the rooster down at a single gulp. This will free me from the curse under which I now live.

"Help me, beautiful Princess, and as soon as I have finished with the wizard, I will return to my rightful form, in which you now see me. Then I shall ask you to become my bride."

The Princess felt herself falling in love with Niilo as he spoke, so she promised to do everything he asked.

When morning came, the wizard approached the castle of the King, Aslo, and asked if he might buy the Princess' golden ring. He offered the surprised King ten thousand roubles.

The King called the Princess to his side. He told her that if she would sell the ring, he would buy her a ring with three rubies to take its place, and give her a lot of money besides. The Princess refused, but she was forced to take the ring from her finger. In handing it to the King, she made sure to drop it, as she had promised Niilo. Just as predicted, the ring rolled into a corner and turned into a heap of green peas.

The wizard instantly changed himself into a rooster,

but before he knew what was happening, Niilo cried out a charm:

Minä revoksi, sinä revon syötiksi.

I a fox, you the fox's food.

And as he spoke, he turned into a fox, and swallowed the rooster at a single gulp.

When Niilo again stood before them, a handsome young man, the King was at first afraid to let his daughter marry him, because of Niilo's magic. But the Princess pleaded with her father, telling him how dearly she and Niilo loved each other, and very soon he changed his mind. He called all his people together, and for two whole weeks they celebrated the marriage of Niilo and the Princess with feasting and with song.

As for Niilo, he had his fill of magic by now and was glad enough to have done with it for good and all. For not all the magic in the world was so wonderful to him as his wonderful bride.

URHO AND MARJA

There was once a King named Arvo. He lived with his wife in a beautiful castle by the sea, but they were very sad, for they had no children nor were ever likely to have any.

To ease his heart, the King set out on a long voyage across the sea. All went well until one day the ship ran aground upon a sandy shoal. With all their might the sailors labored to free the ship, but the harder they worked, the firmer their ship settled into the sand.

Just as they were about to give up hope, a Sea God with a bushy green beard and shining green eyes lifted his head above the water and said to the King:

"If you will give me whatever is born in your home while you are away on this voyage, I will free your ship. If you will not give me what is born, you will never escape as long as the winds blow and the moon shines on the water."

The King thought to himself:

"In my absence perhaps a calf or a lamb has been born."

He answered the Sea God:

"Free my boat, and it shall be as you wish."

The Sea God caused the sand to disappear, and the King sailed back to his kingdom.

When the King approached the castle, his wife came running to greet him. In one arm she carried a baby boy and in the other a baby girl.

The King was at first overjoyed, but soon he remembered his promise to the Sea God, and was sad.

He said nothing to his wife about this promise, but took his servants into the deep wild forest and built a *tupa* in the midst of a dense clump of fir trees, so that the Sea God could not find it. Here he took his children, and left them in the care of his trusted servants.

After a few years, the Sea God came to the King and said:

"Do you remember your promise to me?"

"I do," replied the King.

The King then sent his servants, and they brought a cow, a sheep, and a horse.

"These were born while I was away," said the King, "and I have kept them for you."

The Sea God was very angry, and cried out:

"Give me the boy and the girl according to your promise!"

Then the King sent his servants to the *tupa* of a poor man of the village, and gave him money for two of his children. These he gave to the Sea God.

The Sea God took the children to his palace under the sea, where there is never day, and never night, but always a soft green twilight. There the Sea God began to question the children.

"Since you are the children of a King," he said, "tell me what is the sweetest of the sweet."

"That is honey," answered the children.

"And what is softest of the soft?"

"The side of a feather," answered the children.

"And what is hardest of the hard?"

"Stone," they said, "that is the hardest of the hard."

"The King has deceived me," said the Sea God as he twisted his long green beard in anger. "You are not the children of the King."

He took the peasant's children, one under each arm, and returned to the King's palace.

"These are not your children," he said. "You have hidden your children. Tell me where I can find them."

The King refused to tell, and none of the servants dared say a word. The Sea God's eyes grew darker and darker with anger, and he twisted his scraggly green beard into a knot.

"Tell me," he said, "where you have hidden the children."

No one spoke, until at last a stool in the corner spoke in a dry, squeaky voice:

"The King always kicks me. He cannot treat me worse, even if I tell. Take me upon your shoulder, O Sea God, and I will help you to find the place where the children are hidden."

The Sea God took the stool upon his shoulder, and the stool directed him to the *tupa* in the midst of a dense clump of fir trees.

As soon as the Sea God found the King's children, he began to question them.

"What is the sweetest of the sweet?"

"Mother's milk," they answered.

"What is the softest of the soft?"

"Mother's lap."

"And what is the hardest of the hard?"

"Father's heart," they answered, "that is the hardest of the hard."

"Now I know that you are the children of the King," answered the Sea God. "What are your names?"

"Marja," answered the girl.

"Urho," answered the boy.

"Come with me, Marja and Urho," laughed the Sea God as he clasped their hands in his long green fingers. "I will not hurt you. Come with me to my palace under the sea."

As they started, the Sea God began to sing a song. It sounded like the ripple of cool water over pebbles. The children looked at the cold green eyes of the Sea God, and at the shining scales that covered his body, but his song was so lovely that they were not at all afraid.

When they came to the sea shore, the Sea God took them upon his broad green back, and swam under the waves. Soon they were in the kingdom below the sea. A soft green light surrounded them. On every side stretched meadows with slowly waving fronds.

"What is this place?" Urho asked.

"This is my kingdom under the sea," answered the Sea God.

They walked through forests of tall seaweed that swayed back and forth with the waves. Curious fish swam about and gazed at the children with wide transparent eyes, and these eyes glowed with a cold light like the light of glow worms.

The children began to feel frightened, but once more the Sea God sang. This time his song was like the murmur of the sleepy waves upon the sand.

Soon they reached the Sea God's palace. The castle was made of deep rose coral, and its wide doors were of shining pearl. About the palace was a glistening fence, woven of long, shining golden eels.

"Here you will be very happy," said the Sea God.

Years passed in this kingdom under the sea. Urho learned to ride upon the backs of shining fishes, and to hunt for strange treasures around the coral reefs. Marja tended the garden, where grew curious flowers that looked like pale blue and yellow sea shells.

The years passed slowly under the sea, but Marja grew into a beautiful young princess. When the Sea God saw how each day she became more beautiful, he fell in love with her.

"Be my wife," said the Sea God, "and all the riches in my kingdom shall be yours."

Marja looked at his cold green eyes, and at his scraggly green beard, and at the fish-like scales that covered his body.

"If only the Sea God were beautiful like my brother Urho," said Marja to herself, "I would gladly marry him."

Urho saw what was happening. He had long since grown restless and lonely for the stars and the sun and the wind and the sky. One day as he was riding on a fish, he had come very near to the top of the sea, so that the sunlight had touched his face. Since that day Urho had been lonely and homesick in this cold kingdom.

"If only I could escape and find my way back to the upper world and to my father's castle, I would be happy," he sighed.

One day as Urho sat alone in the sea-weed forest he looked up at the waving green fronds and thought of the firs that swayed toward the skies in his father's country.

He began to weep, and without warning he heard a voice speaking to him in his own language. He looked up and saw a great shaggy wolf.

"Why do you weep?" asked the wolf. "I have come from the upper world to take you back to your father's castle. Climb on my back."

"I will gladly come," answered Urho, "but I have a sister. I must take her with me."

"Fetch her then," said the wolf, "and I will wait for you here.

Urho ran into the castle, caught Marja in his arms, and leapt upon the wolf's back. The wolf began to run along the bottom of the sea.

"When you see the Sea God coming," said the wolf, "tell me."

After a short time, Urho shouted:

"Make haste! The Sea God is coming!"

"Lift my right ear," said the wolf. "Under it you will find a pebble. Throw the pebble behind you and shout this charm:

'Elköhöt pääsko siivin lentäjät, jaloin juoksijat ylitse, ei ympäritse, päitse eikä päällitse (Let there not pass over

[152]

you, under you, nor through you, any creature with wings nor any runner on foot) .' "

Urho lifted the pebble from beneath the Wolf's ear, threw it behind him, and repeated the charm. Instantly a mountain of stone appeared that reached to the very top of the waves and beyond them toward the sky.

When the Sea God reached the mountain of stone, he had to return to his castle for a pickaxe. He came back quickly, and chopped a hole through the mountain. He was hiding his pickaxe behind a stone, when a tiny perch swam past him and said in a squeaky little voice:

"I see you!"

"Ka!" said the Sea God, "that perch will tell his larger brothers, and they will steal my pickaxe if I leave it here. I must take it back to my palace."

The Sea God carried his pickaxe back, and again took up the chase. He swam so fast through the water that he soon overtook the running wolf, captured Marja and Urho, and carried them back to his home.

The Sea God now decided that he must charm Marja so that she would love him, and not want to go back to her parents. Whereupon he called together all the fishes of the sea.

"My friends," he cried to them, "tell me how I may win Marja for my bride!"

None of them knew, it seemed, until at last a very large swordfish spoke in a hoarse voice:

"In the distant meadows of the sea there is a white flower shaped like a five pointed star. Take this flower, place it in your Marja's golden hair, and she will straightway fall in love with you."

"But where can I find this flower?" asked the Sea God.

"We will help you," cried the fishes, and they set out

[153]

swimming in all directions. But after many days the fishes, one by one, returned. None of them had been able to find the flower. Just as the King was ready to give up in despair, a tiny minnow flickered down through the waves. In its mouth was a shining white flower that sparkled like a star.

The Sea God thanked all the fishes, and took the flower to Marja. He found her lying upon a couch set with mother-of-pearl, weeping because she, too, wished to return to her old home.

The Sea God placed the flower in Marja's hair, and she straightway fell in love with him. Now she gladly stayed in the Sea God's palace, for the flower had worked its spell upon her.

"If you only knew how much I love you," the Sea God said again and again to Marja, "you would become my wife."

"I will become your wife when another year has passed," said Marja, "for I, too, love you."

Again Urho saw what was happening. He walked into the garden among the flowers, and sat under a tall waving frond. As he wept he once more heard a voice in the language he knew. He looked up and saw before him a reindeer with great antlers.

"Why are you unhappy?" said the reindeer.

"I am far from my father's castle in the Upper World."

"I have come from the Upper World to save you," replied the reindeer. "Climb on my back, and I will take you to your home."

"I cannot go without my sister," said Urho. "I dare not leave her, for she is under the spell of the Sea God."

"Fetch her along," answered the reindeer, "I will wait for you here."

When Urho placed Marja upon the reindeer's back, she began to cry. "Do not take me from the Sea God. He is kind to me, and I love him."

Urho did not listen to his sister.

"The Sea God has bewitched you, Marja," he said. "We must fly back to our father's castle."

Urho held Marja before him on the reindeer's back, and the great beast leapt forward, along the pale sands under the sea.

After a long time the reindeer said to Urho:

"If you see the Sea God coming, let me know, and I will tell you what to do."

Urho looked, and after a while saw the Sea God running after them. He shouted to the reindeer.

"Take a handful of hair from my mane, and throw it behind you," said the reindeer. "Repeat this charm:

'*Elköhöt pääskössiivin lentäjät* (Appear bush mountain. Rise toward the heavens. Let not pass over you, through you, nor under you, any creature winged nor runner on foot).'"

Urho did as he was bid, and there rose a great mountain of brush that reached from the bottom of the sea to the top of the waves, and upward toward the skies. It was so thick not even the sun could shine through it nor under it.

When the Sea God found that he could not pass the brush mountain, he swam back to his palace for a spade. He hastened to the brush mountain, dug a tunnel under the mountain, and was about to hurry after the travellers, when the perch who had watched him hide the spade under a rock cried:

"I see you!"

Again the Sea God was afraid the perch would steal

[155]

his tool. He carried the spade back to the palace, and then hurried after the brother and sister. He overtook them just as they were about to reach the upper world, and carried them back to his palace.

Another year passed, and Marja and the Sea God were making ready for their wedding feast. Urho could do nothing but weep to see how Marja had been bewitched.

One day when he was alone crying, a fox sprang up before him, and began speaking to him in his own language.

"Why do you weep?" asked the fox.

"I am far from my father's castle, and the Sea God has bewitched my sister, Marja."

"I heard you sobbing as I wandered about in the pine forests of the Upper World," said the fox, "and I have come to save you. Bring your sister, Marja, with you, and I will carry you both to your father's castle."

Urho set his sister on the fox's back against her will, and the fox slipped slyly out of sight before the Sea God knew that anything was happening.

After a long time, the fox said to Urho:

"If you see the Sea God coming, tell me."

At last Urho saw the Sea God swimming toward them, and told the fox.

The fox said:

"Under my left ear you will find a fire brand. Hurl it behind you, and repeat this charm:

'*Nouse, tuli vouri* (Rise, mountain of flame. Allow no living creature to pass, neither a bird with wings, a beast with feet, a fish with fins, nor a creeping or crawling worm).'"

Urho did as he was bid, and there rose a mountain of fire so high that its head lifted into the Upper World, and its arms clasped the shore. This time the Sea God could do nothing. He stood before the flame and wept like a helpless child.

After the fox had taken Marja and Urho into the Upper World Urho decided to rest for a day or two, and build a *tupa* in the edge of the deep wild forest.

The fox said to Urho:

"Will you not let me live with you?"

"Gladly I will," answered Urho, "for you have helped me escape the power of the Sea God."

The next day came the wolf and the reindeer, and they, too, wanted to live with Urho. They were all happy except Marja. She kept her eyes constantly fixed on the mountain of fire, and sighed for her missing Sea God.

One day Urho went into the deep forest with the wolf, the reindeer, and the fox to hunt. While they were away, Marja ran to the mountain of fire with her broom. She swept earth upon the rearing flame, and put it out.

As soon as the fire was out, the Sea God climbed over the mountain, and Marja brought him with her to the *tupa*. They were happy until they heard Urho and his three companions returning.

"You must hide yourself," said Marja, "for my brother will make trouble if he finds you here."

"That is easy," said the Sea God. "I will change myself into a needle, and then you can place me in a crack between the logs. When Urho returns to the forest tomorrow with his companions, I will hop out and be myself again."

As soon as Urho and his companions saw that the mountain of fire was no longer burning, they said to Marja:

[157]

"Where is the Sea God? He must be near."

"How should I know where he is?" said Marja.

"We'll soon find him," said the Fox, the Wolf, and the Reindeer, "for we know he is here," and they began to tear down the walls of the *tupa*.

"Won't you leave me even a room for my head?" Marja cried, and they had to stop.

Next morning Marja said:

"Brother Urho, I am very sick. Unless you and your companions fetch me the magic brew that is hidden behind the nine doors at the bottom of the sea, I fear that I shall die."

Urho and his three companions knew that the Sea God had told Marja to say this. The Fox, the Wolf, and the Reindeer, however, hurried off to fetch the magic brew, but they left Urho to hide behind a tree, so that he could see all that happened.

When Urho had waited a little while he saw the needle leap from between the logs, and turn itself into the Sea God.

"This is a good joke," laughed the Sea God, as he stroked Marja's golden hair with his long green fingers. "Now we shall have peace. Your brother and his three companions will never find the end of their journey. They will trouble us no more. Come, let us make merry."

Urho became so angry that he opened the door of the *tupa* and shouted:

"Sea God, it is time for us to settle our differences alone. Come with me into the deep wild forest."

"As you will," said the Sea God.

Urho and the Sea God disappeared among the trees, and Marja sat down and wept.

[158]

Meanwhile, the Fox, the Wolf, and the Reindeer sped on their long journey and at last came to the kingdom of the Sea God. There they found a deserted castle on a far meadow. The nine great iron doors of the castle stood wide open. They rushed in to find the magic brew, and just as they lifted the jar from his place in the corner, the great doors creaked on their rusty hinges, and closed with a clang. The three companions found themselves prisoners.

"We must not lose heart," said the fox, "for Urho has need of us."

They began digging through the floor of the castle with their sharp claws, and after a long time found themselves free once more.

When they reached the *tupa* with the jar of magic brew Marja was still weeping bitterly.

"Why are you sad?" asked the Fox as he placed the medicine in Marja's hand.

"I am sure that both my brother and my lover are dead. They went into the deep wild forest long days ago to fight, and have not returned."

"We shall find them," said the three companions.

The Fox, the Wolf, and the Reindeer hurried into the forest, and after a long search, they found Urho lying on his back under a great fir tree.

"I see what has happened," whispered the wily Fox. "The Sea God has changed himself into a needle, and has thrust himself into Urho's head. Let us see if we cannot trick the Sea God. We'll lie down, and make believe that we are asleep. I will lie nearest the needle, for the Sea God hates me most."

The three companions did as the Fox suggested. When the Sea God thought that the Fox was fast asleep,

[159]

he leapt at him. The wily Fox jerked his head aside, and the needle buried itself deep in the side of the fir tree. The fir tree at once turned brown and withered, but the needle was held fast.

Urho sat up, rubbed his eyes open, and said:

"How long have I been sleeping?"

The three companions told him all that had happened.

"We must hurry back to the *tupa*," said Urho. "Now that the Sea God is buried in the fir tree, Marja will forget him and be happy."

When Urho and his companions reached the *tupa*, they found Marja still weeping her heart out.

"You must come with us, Marja," said Urho. "We are going back to the home of our childhood."

Marja wanted to stay, but Urho and his companions led her by the hand. When at last they reached their father's kingdom they saw a church. As they entered it, the spell of the Sea God fell from Marja, and she forgot her lost lover.

Urho and Marja found the King and the Queen in the palace still mourning for their long lost children. The King's hard heart had been softened by his sorrow.

After Urho and Marja told their parents all that had happened, the King made a great feast, and invited all the people of his kingdom to celebrate the return of his children. As for the Fox, the Wolf, and the Reindeer, they ate from the golden dishes of the King's own table. And they all lived happily ever after.

MIELIKKI AND HER NINE SONS

Once upon a time three maidens were walking through the deep wild forest, chattering gaily as maidens will.

"From three barley seeds," said the first maiden, "I can make bread for an army."

"That is nothing," laughed the second, "for from three stalks of flax, I can make clothes for an army."

Mielikki, the third maiden, was silent, and after thinking for a while she said:

"It seems to me much more wonderful that I can become the mother of nine sons."

Now, Aslo, the King of the country, was riding through the woods at the time, and he overheard all that the maidens said. He was so charmed with Mielikki's beauty and by her serious words, that he leapt from his horse, knelt at her feet, and asked her to be his wife.

Mielikki consented, the King set her before him on the saddle, and they rode off together to his castle.

Time passed, and it happened that Mielikki was about to give birth to three beautiful sons. The King was so proud that he made a feast, and called his people together to help him celebrate. Among them were two singers who sat on benches opposite one another, interlocked their fingers, and began to sing, while a third old man played on the *kantele.* They sang of the beauty of the queen, and the courage of the King, and at last they sang of the three sons who would be born:

> Hands golden from the wrist,
> Feet silver from the knee,
> Shining dawn from the shoulder,
> Moonbeams from the breast,
> Stars of the heavens from the forehead,
> Three such handsome sons, such noble sons,
> Our King shall have.

When the feast was over, the King sent his servant to seek a midwife. As the servant walked along the road, he met Noita-Akka, an old witch in disguise, who asked:

"My good man, where do you go?"

"To seek a midwife for the King's three young sons," answered the servant truthfully, for he did not know that the woman was a witch.

"Take me," said the Noita-Akka, "for I am skilled in bringing children into the world."

"Very well," replied the servant, "come with me."

"But first I must stop at my *tupa,*" said the witch. "Wait here a few minutes till I return, and I will gladly go with you."

The servant waited, and the old witch hastened into the forest, took three black crows, who were her own sons, hid them away in the folds of her apron, and returned with the servant to the castle.

[162]

When no one was watching, the witch exchanged her three black crows for the King's three beautiful children, whom she hid away in the forest.

The old witch then brought the three crows to the King and said with a snarl:

"Ka! I came to care for three children, and I find three black crows!"

The King was filled with horror, but he answered:

"To be sure, you must care for these."

The joy of the castle was changed to sadness, and the King and Mielikki lived with the three crows without knowing that they had been tricked by Noita-Akka.

After many months, Mielikki again told the King that she was ready to present him with three more sons.

It happened that Noita-Akka had again three newborn sons who were crows, and these she wished to have raised as Princes. She changed her appearance, and again hired herself to Mielikki as a midwife. And when the King's three beautiful sons were born, she substituted her three black crows, and hid the rightful children behind a white stone on a grassy glade in the deep wild wood.

The King was completely deceived by the witch, and was very sorrowful. He was sorely disappointed with Mielikki.

A third time Mielikki was ready to present the King with three sons, and again the King sent his servant to seek a midwife.

Noita-Akka this time completely changed her appearance so that the servant did not know her when he met her along the road. She again asked:

"Whither do you go?"

"To seek a midwife for the King's wife, Mielikki."

"Hire me, for I am skillful in bringing children into the world," said the witch.

And so the servant hired Noita-Akka, the witch, for the third time.

It happened that two sons were already born before Noita-Akka arrived, and these Mielikki hid beside her in the bed, for she feared the midwife had tricked her before.

The witch was deceived, and believed that there was only one son born. This son she changed for her three black crows, and hid the King's child away behind the white stone in the forest.

The King was now at his wit's end. He believed that Mielikki, despite her beauty, must be an evil spirit from Hiitola (the dominions of the Evil Power). And he became frightened lest she should work an evil charm upon him. He therefore commanded that she be placed in an iron barrel, given food for thirteen years, and cast adrift upon the open sea.

Mielikki hid her two beautiful sons in the folds of her shawl, and for thirteen years was tossed about in the barrel upon the tides, and driven about by the winds.

But at last a strange thing happened. The barrel burst open, and Mielikki and her two sons. who had by this time grown to young manhood, found themselves upon a rocky island in the midst of the sea.

They were afraid they would perish, for there was no food upon the island. And then one day a great sturgeon swam to the shore and said:

"Cut open my side."

"Indeed I will not," said Martti, the larger son.

"Cut open my side," repeated the sturgeon. "Do as I

[164]

tell you, and you will find a blue patch of cloth and a white handkerchief. When you wave the blue patch in the form of a cross over the ground, there will arise by magic a beautiful palace. And if you wave the blue patch over the sea, a bridge of stone will rise from this island to the mainland."

"And what about the white handkerchief?" asked Olavi, the smaller son.

"Carry the handkerchief in the bottom of your pocket," said the sturgeon, "for you will need that another time."

Martti and Olavi did as they were bid, and by magic a palace of shining gold stood before them, while a bridge of stone stretched for many miles from the very door of the palace to the garden of Mielikki's husband, King Aslo.

When the lords and ladies of the King's court saw the bridge rise by magic out of the sea, they wondered where it led. But they did not dare to cross it, for they feared it might be the work of evil spirits.

It happened that at this time a beggar came to the King's palace for food. When he saw the strange bridge, he became curious and started to cross it. After long hours, footsore and weary, he came to the island where dwelt Mielikki and her two sons.

They took the beggar into their palace, set him down at their golden table, and fed him such food as he had never before tasted. When he was ready to leave, Martti and Olavi filled his pockets with treasures of gold and jewels.

Then the beggar again returned to the castle of the King, where he told Aslo of the fabulous wealth of the island.

"If you only saw that island," he said to the King,

"you would no longer sit here looking sadly on the sea."

"How do you reach this island?" the King asked.

"Follow the great stone bridge, and after a long time you will hear the song of birds, and see the glittering golden palace. Within the castle dwells a lovely woman, with sad eyes. Two beautiful sons she has, and when you look upon them, you will think of the old song of the bards:

> Hands golden from the wrist,
> Feet silver from the knee,
> Shining dawn from the shoulder,
> Moonbeams from the breast,
> Stars of the heavens from the forehead—

The song recalled old memories, and the King began to sigh and wonder if this might not be Mielikki, his wife, whom he had set adrift in a barrel on the open sea.

The King said: "Take me to see this wondrous island with my own eyes."

The beggar led the King across the bridge, and when they reached the island, they were greeted by Martti and Olavi.

"From what land did you come hither?" asked King Aslo.

"Our mother never told us," answered Martti. "The first land we ever knew was this island. Most of our life has been spent in an iron barrel."

When the King heard this tale, his heart was heavy. He said:

"I am the cause of all your trouble, for I feared your mother was an evil spirit from Hiitola, and I set her to perish on the open seas. But now you must take me to your mother."

The King was so happy to find Mielikki that he took

her and her two sons with him back to his castle. As they stepped upon the bridge, Martti waved the blue patch over the ground. The palace mysteriously disappeared, and only green trees remained. After they had crossed the stone bridge, Martti waved the blue patch over the water, and the long arches vanished into air.

The King was so joyous over the return of Mielikki that he called all his people together and celebrated with a great feast.

When they were alone again, Martti said to his mother:

"Why is it that Olavi and I have no brothers?"

"You have seven brothers," said Mielikki, "but they were stolen away by the Noita-Akka, the witch, when they were born."

"Then we must go to seek them," said Martti.

When Mielikki saw that her two sons were determined to go in quest of their lost brothers, she took drops of milk from her own breasts, mixed the milk with flour, and baked loaves of *rieska* (unleavened bread), and gave them to Martti and Olavi with her blessing.

The boys put the bread in their knapsacks and set out upon their journey. After a few days they saw, high in a tree top, a sea gull with shining plumage.

"Let us shoot this bird," said Olavi.

"It is more beautiful alive," replied Martti.

While they argued, they were astonished to hear the bird speaking in their own language.

"Do not shoot me," called the gull, "spare my life, and I will reward you."

Olavi, who had drawn his bow, did not shoot, and after a few minutes the bird flew away.

At the end of another day, Martti and Olavi came to the seashore.

[167]

"Where shall we go now?" asked Olavi.

"If you had shot the gull, we would not be here," answered Martti. "The bird has brought us bad luck."

"But it promised to come to our aid," said Olavi.

As they talked, they heard a flapping of wings, and a great gray bird alighted on the beach beside them.

"Sit upon my back," said the bird. "I will take you across the sea."

Almost before they were aware of it, they found themselves on the back of the great bird, far out over the blue sea. After a long flight they came to a strange country. Here the bird alighted, the boys climbed to the ground.

"What shall we do next?" asked Olavi. "We are lost and far from home."

"But I still have the white handkerchief in the bottom of my pocket where the sturgeon told me to carry it," said Martti.

As Martti drew the white handkerchief from his pocket, a light breeze snatched it from his hand and carried it a few feet into the air.

Martti and Olavi both ran to catch it, but the faster they ran, the faster the handkerchief floated before them. Soon they saw that this was a magic piece of linen, and that it was given them to be their guide.

They had not followed it far before they saw a strange, glowing, copper-colored bird in a tree before them. The bird called:

"Where are you going, my boys?"

"We go to seek our brothers," said Martti. "Can you help us to find them?"

"I know nothing of your brothers," answered the bird, "but if you ask the old woman in the hut just over the hill yonder, perhaps she can tell you something."

The boys thanked the bird, and hurried forward. They entered the hut, and found the old woman, bent and feeble, spinning wool beside the hearth.

"Who are you, and where are you going?" asked the old woman in a weak voice, stopping her wheel so that she might hear the answer.

"We are the sons of Aslo, the King, and of Mielikki, the Queen," said Martti, "and we seek our seven lost brothers over land and sea."

"You will find them in the far Northland," said the old woman. "Follow the white handkerchief to the next house, and the old woman who lives there can tell you what to do."

The boys thanked the old woman, and did as they were bid. They found the house, and knocked upon the door, for it was barred. Another old woman, twice as bent and feeble as the first, opened the door, and said:

"Who are you and what do you seek?"

"We are sons of Mielikki, the Queen, and Aslo, the King," said Olavi, "and we are in quest of our seven lost brothers."

"You are at your journey's end," said the old woman. "Your brothers spend each night here as men. But each day they fly as gulls over the sea. Before entering the house, they leave their robes of white feathers beneath these pines. There is but one way that you can save your brothers. Hide under the trees, and when you see them enter the house, seize the robes, carry them away and burn them so that not one feather remains. They will then walk the earth as humans for the rest of their lives."

Martti and Olavi hid themselves as they had been bid. At twilight they heard the swish of moving wings, and the next minute saw seven great birds alight. And then they saw their seven brothers discard their robes of feathers and enter the house.

Martti and Olavi lost no time in gathering the feathers together and setting fire to them.

When the smoke entered the house, the seven brothers ran outside and cried:

"Why do you burn our robes? Now we can never again leave the earth and fly into the skies!"

"Do you not know us?" shouted Martti. "We are your brothers come to break the spell of Noita-Akka, the witch."

But the seven sons had been gulls ever since they were small children, and knew nothing of the spell under which they lived.

At last Martti and Olavi broke the loaves of their mother's unleavened bread into seven pieces. And when the brothers tasted their mother's milk, the spell of the witch was broken, and they remembered their mother, and longed to go back to their old home.

Martti and Olavi gladly led the way, following the magic white handkerchief. After many days, when they reached the castle of their parents, the handkerchief changed into a white moth and flew away.

Since Noita-Akka had died, there was no one else who wished evil upon the King and Mielikki and her nine sons. And so from this time forward, they all lived happily together.

LEPPÄ POLKKY AND THE BLUE CROSS

There was once a man, named Jukka. He and his wife were sorely troubled because no child had come to bless their home. But even in their old age they did not give up hope. They went into the deep forest, found an alder stump, and placed it in the waiting cradle. For three years they rocked the cradle gently, but nothing happened. Then one day while the father was plowing in the field and the mother was milking the cows, a wizard, passing by, changed the alder stump into a boy.

That evening when Jukka and his wife came home for supper, there was the boy walking across the floor. He called:

"Mother, give me bread."

"At last our wish has come true," cried Jukka.

Years passed, and the boy grew by leaps and bounds into manhood. He was taller by a head than other men, and his muscles were of iron. The people of the village called him Leppä Pölkky, which means "alder stump."

One day it happened that darkness suddenly covered the whole earth. The King in Leppä's country sent forth his soldiers to find a wise man who could tell how to bring back the dawn, the moonlight, and sunshine to the world. At last a Laplander wizard was found, who came to the King's castle and told the King that an evil witch, Loviatar, with her three serpent sons, had pulled the moon, the sun, and the dawn out of the sky, and imprisoned them in the sea. Thus it was that the world was always in darkness.

The wizard also told the King that he must find three men strong enough to journey to the farthest north, to bring the dawn, the moon, and the sun back again. He told the King to test the men by seeing how much strong wine they could drink.

Once more the King sent his heralds throughout the land, and at last two men were found stronger than all the others. One of these men could drink three bottles of wine, the other, six.

"We yet need a man who can drink nine bottles of wine," said the King.

The King's messengers searched everywhere, but they found no man who could drink more than six bottles. So the King called the Laplander wizard to him again, and asked his advice.

"There is no man but Leppä Pölkky in all your kingdom," replied the wizard, "who can drink nine bottles of your powerful wine."

The King then ordered Leppä Pölkky to be brought

before him. And Leppä Pölkky gulped down nine bottles of the wine as if it were water, and asked for more.

The King was satisfied, and gave each of the three strong men a horse, a dog, and money for the journey. He asked each to carry as many bottles of the wine as he could drink.

"You will need these bottles in your time of trial," said the King. "So don't waste them along the way."

After the King had blessed the three men, the three horses, and the three wolfhounds, Leppä Pölkky and his companions set off through the darkness to rescue the moon and the sun from their grave in the sea. At the end of many days, *Päivänkoitto,* the dawn, began to glimmer faintly. They took hope and rode faster until they saw a feeble reflection of *Kuu,* the moon. But they did not stop until they met *Aurinko,* the sun, above the edge of the sea.

Presently they came to the home of the wise widow, Leski-Akka. She was seated in a hut made of the skins of polar bears.

"*Ka,* how is it that you have sunlight here, while the rest of the world is dark?" the men asked the widow.

"O-ho, my lads," she answered, "the day is not always golden here, either. The Paha-Sydamiset, the evil-hearted sons of the old witch Loviatar, have put a curse on the day. They are all thieves, and cannot steal in the light. When they go into the sea they take the sun, the moon and the dawn with them. Then it becomes night, and we do not see the sun again until they return to shore."

"Who is this old witch Loviatar?" Leppa asked.

"You from Finland should know her," said the widow. "It is she who brought the nine sicknesses to Finland.

[173]

These wicked sons of hers who steal the dawn, the moon and the sun are three serpents even more evil-hearted than their ugly mother."

The three men walked on. Presently they saw a castle, one half of which wept while the other half laughed. This amazed them, and they went back to Leski-Akka to ask what the strange sight could mean.

"It is like this," said Leski-Akka. "The King of our country has just taken his eldest daughter as a sacrifice to the three-headed serpent, Loviatar's eldest son. This he must do, for otherwise the serpent will destroy one half of the castle, one half of the people, and one half of the shining jewels. If any man could slay the monster, then once more would dawn rise over the world."

"I will try my strength to make an end of this three-headed serpent," answered the man who could drink the three bottles.

When they were again alone, the three-bottle drinker said to his companions:

"If, in fighting, I let fly my boot toward you, loose the three dogs we brought with us to help me."

He drank three bottles of wine to strengthen his courage, and rode off alone to slay the monster.

On the shore of the sea he found the serpent, and fought with it. When he was hard pressed, he let fly his boot, and his companions loosed the three dogs. The fight grew more and more furious, but in the end the three-headed serpent, the first son of Loviatar, the witch, lay dead; and dawn had begun to spread over the whole earth.

When it was dark again, the three men walked once more toward the King's castle. Again one half of the castle wept and the other half laughed. They hurried back to Leski-Akka, and the man who could drink six bottles asked:

"Why does one side of the castle again weep, and the other side laugh? Did we not kill the three-headed serpent?"

"*Oi* (oh) my boy!" answered Leski-Akka. "The six-headed serpent, the second son of the witch, now threatens to destroy one half of the castle, one half of the people, and one half of the shining jewels. To prevent this, the King has just taken his second daughter as a sacrifice. If a man were found strong enough to slay the monster, not only would the king's daughter be saved, but moonlight and dreams would return to the earth."

"I will make an end to this six-headed monster," answered the man who could drink six bottles.

When they were alone in the garden, he said:

"If you see my boot fly, loose the dogs to aid me."

He then drank the six bottles, and rode off with courage to slay the monster.

The next day the silver moon shone around the whole world, and the six-bottle man rode back to the castle with the second daughter of the King.

A third time the men walked in the garden, and once again they saw the strange sight. One side of the castle wept, the other laughed. For the third time the men returned to Leski-Akka. This time it was Leppä Pölkky who asked:

"Why does one part of the castle still weep and the other laugh?"

"This is the truth of the matter," said Leski-Akka. "The King has just taken his youngest daughter as a sacrifice to the third son of the witch, the nine-headed monster. He has threatened to devour half the castle with its people and wealth. If a man could be found strong enough to kill this most terrible of the three sons of the ogress, the sun would shine upon the earth, and again day would be golden."

"I shall see what I can do," answered Leppä.

When the three men were alone, Leppä told his two companions, if they saw his boot fly through the air, to loose the three dogs to aid him. He then gulped down the nine bottles of wine, and rode off without fear on his fiery steed to slay the monster.

There was dawn and moonlight over all the world, but the sun still lay hidden in the sea. For a long while the people waited, until they almost gave up hope.

Then, suddenly, to the joy of all, golden day flowed over the earth, and Leppä came riding from the seashore with the King's youngest daughter unharmed.

The King was so grateful to these brave men who had slain the three terrible serpent sons of Loviatar, that he gave a great feast, and in the midst of the rejoicing, he said to Leppä Pölkky and his two companions:

"My distinguished guests, I desire to give each of you the daughter of mine whom he has saved. The half of my castle and gold and jewels will I also divide with you if you will make your home with me."

The three brave men bowed low to the King, and Leppä answered for all of them:

"We thank you, O King, for your gracious hospitality! We are sorry that we cannot accept your gifts, but we have come as messengers from another King who dwells far away from this country. To him we are pledged to return. If you will give us meat and drink for our journey homeward, we shall ask no more."

The King gave Leppä and his two companions food for

Together they rode happily back

their journey, and they set out for home. Through moonlight, dawn and day they rode, for the journey was long.

Presently they saw a hut of willow boughs by the road side. Within they could hear harsh voices quarrelling. It was Loviatar and her witch cronies. Leppä crept to the window to listen.

"The men who killed my three sons are coming down the road," Loviatar raged. "They think they'll get home safely, but destroy them I will!"

Leppä turned cold with fright, for the witches were the ugliest hags he had ever seen. They had long yellow teeth and finger nails of iron, and Loviatar's face was a deep purple.

A second witch cried in a shrill voice: "You cannot do this, old Loviatar! They are too strong for you."

"I will put the spell of hunger on them," Loviatar screamed. "When they are starving I will set tables of rich food before them, and when they stop to eat I'll catch them."

"But suppose they think to strike a cross on the table with their sword?" jeered another witch. "Then your spell would be broken."

"Then I'll charm them with thirst. I'll set a sparkling pool before them, and destroy them when they stoop to drink."

"But if they cut the pool with two sword strokes in the form of a cross, then they'd escape you!"

"I'll burden them with sleep, and set beds for them," Loviatar screeched. "That way I'll catch them surely!"

"Unless they break the charm by striking the beds with their sword!"

"They will never know how to break my charms unless one of you witches tells them," shouted Loviatar furiously, "and whoever reveals these words of mine shall be changed into a blue cross!"

When he heard all this, Leppä hurried back to his companions.

"What were they quarrelling about?" his companions asked.

Leppä did not dare to tell, for fear he should be changed into a blue cross forthwith. He answered:

"They were quarrelling over nothing at all, as all old women do."

The three men mounted their horses, but before they had gone very far they were taken with a great hunger. It seemed that they could not go another step for weakness. At that very moment they saw before them a table all set with food and drink.

Leppä jumped to the ground and struck the table three strokes with his sword, in the form of a cross, and instantly the table vanished.

His two comrades were very angry. They began to abuse Leppä, but he dared not tell them the truth for fear of the witch's spell. He said:

"What do we want with food—our hunger has left us. Food will taste far better when we reach our journey's end."

Again they rode, and now a great thirst came upon them. They saw a pool of sparkling water with three birch bark dippers set beside it.

The two men jumped from their horses, but Leppä was quicker still. He struck the water with his sword and the pool vanished, and with it their thirst. But the two men were nearly beside themselves with rage. Leppä said:

"We have no need of water. In our own country we

[179]

can find the best and the clearest water in the world."

They rode on, farther and still farther. And now a great drowsiness overcame them, till they were ready to drop from the saddle for sheer weariness. And there by the wayside they saw three comfortable beds.

Leppä sprang from his horse, and slashed one bed with three strokes of his sword. It disappeared, but before he could touch the other two beds his companions had flung themselves down. And then Loviatar destroyed them before Leppä's very eyes. She stole Leppä's horse and drove it back to the stable beside her hut, and tied it there with an iron chain. Poor Leppä was forced to flee for his life on foot.

Leppä was now alone in the woods, and far from home. He wept for the fate of his two companions as he walked forward, footsore and weary. At last he sat down beside a tree to rest. Here he discovered an eye watching him through a hole in the bark. And as he sat wondering at it, he heard the heart-broken wail of a maiden.

This maiden had come under the power of the old witch, Loviatar, who had blinded her so that she could not find her way. Leppä called the maiden to him, recovered her eye from the tree, and told her who he was. The maiden was so grateful that she led Leppä back to the witch's stable.

"If you strike the chain three blows with your sword in the form of a cross," she whispered, "your horse will be free."

Leppä struck the heavy chain three blows, and it fell to the ground. The witch heard the noise and rushed to the stable. When she saw Leppä with his sword drawn, she shrieked:

"I have a mind to kill you. But I will spare your life

on the one condition, that you will go and bring me Katrina of Kiijoki, the most beautiful princess in the world."

"*Ka*," said Leppä, "get her I will!"

Loviatar then hollowed out a birch log, and gave it to Leppä for a boat. And so there was nothing left for him to do but to set out on the sea in search of the beautiful Katrina.

When he had rowed a short way he heard a man calling from the shore:

"Hoo-hoo! Wherever you are going, Leppä? Take me with you, by God's will!"

Leppä rowed to the shore and asked:

"Who are you among men?"

"Hurttinen-hosuja, the Dog-chaser," the man answered.

"Very well, come along," Leppä replied.

They had rowed but a short distance farther when they heard another man calling:

"Hoo-hoo! Take me with you, Leppä, wherever you are going, by God's will!"

Leppä again rowed to the shore, and asked:

"Who are you?"

"I am Unen-makaaja, the Dream-sleeper."

"Come along," said Leppä.

The three men rowed a little way farther when they heard a call from another part of the shore:

"Take me with you, Leppä, by God's will!"

"And who are you?"

"I am Kylyn-kylpijä, the Bath-bather."

"Come, you are welcome," laughed Leppä.

And now they made a fresh start, but they heard two other men calling:

"Hoo-hoo! Take us with you, Leppä, by God's will!"

One of these was Ruokien-syöjä, the Food-eater, and the other Veden-kantaja, the Water-carrier. These also Leppä took with him.

And now Leppä and his five companions rowed forward as fast as their oars would carry them, and after many hours, they reached Kiijoki.

As their boat scraped the sand, the people saw them coming and set their savage dogs upon them. The dogs snarled and barked with such a din that the men were afraid of being torn to pieces.

Then Leppä said to the first man who had come into the boat:

"Go you, since you are Hurttinen-hosuja, the Dog-chaser, and call off these hounds."

Hurttinen-hosuja leapt from the boat. He waved his hat three times in the air, and the dogs ran in every direction, disappearing as by magic.

Then Leppä and his companions pulled their boat high on the sand and walked bravely into the King's castle. The guards looked at them in wonder, and said:

"You are the first guests who have ever entered this castle. Every time that visitors have come to our shores, our dogs have destroyed them."

"We did not come here to be food for dogs," said Hurttinen-hosuja.

The guards permitted them to enter the castle, and at last they stood before the King. Leppä said:

"I have come from a far country to Kiijoki, to win your beautiful daughter, Katrina."

"If you think she is so easily won, you make a great mistake," answered the King. "First you must sleep away our dreams."

[182]

At this, Unen-makaaja, the Dream-sleeper, stepped forward and answered:

"Gladly we will sleep away your dreams."

The King then asked Leppä and his men to spend the night in his barn. As they stretched upon the floor to sleep, Unen-makaaja covered the men with his body. In the middle of the night, the King sent guards to set fire to the barn. Unen-makaaja slept on top and the burning brands fell upon him, and did the men no harm.

The barn burned to ashes, but the men were not even awakened. When morning came, they all went into the King's castle, and Leppä again spoke to the King:

"You were foolish to try to harm us. See, you have only burned your own barn!"

The King was silent a long time, then he said:

"We will not give Katrina to you unless you first bathe in our bath-house."

"It is as you wish," answered Leppä. "Make the fires hot upon the hearth."

The King commanded his guards to make the *kylpy* (bath) red hot. This was done, but it made little difference. First entered Kylyn-kylpijä, the Bath-bather. He blew his cold breath into the center of the room, and there came by magic a mound of snow, and before the hearth, a pool of water. The bathhouse walls were covered with frost.

After Leppä and his men had bathed, they went together to the King's castle and said:

"You don't treat your guests very well. The stones in the hearth were so cold that there was no steam on the stones for our bath."

Now the King began to be frightened. After a long while he said:

[183]

"We will not give you Katrina in spite of your magic, until you have eaten all the food that we set before you."

"Be it as you wish," said Leppä.

The King called his guards, and commanded them to kill cows and lambs, and to set a huge feast. When the piles were high, Ruokien-syöjä, Food-eater, stepped forward, and alone gulped down all that was set before him. When he had finished, he asked:

"*Ka,* and is this all your food? I am still hungry, and my comrades have had nothing at all."

By this time the King and his people were trembling with fear.

"This is all," they answered. "We have no more grain, and all of our cattle are killed."

Ruokien-syöjä felt sorry for them. He lifted his pack from his shoulders and gave the King and his people a feast.

But the King was still stubborn. When he and all his people had eaten their fill, he grumbled:

"We will not give you our daughter Katrina until first you carry water in a sieve."

It was now the turn of Veden-kantaja, Water-carrier, to step forward:

"Give me a sieve, O King, and I will carry as much water as you wish."

The sieve was brought, and Veden-kantaja took it down to the shore of the sea, filled it with water, and brought it, brimming full, to the King.

When this work was finished, the King and his people talked a long time among themselves.

"*Ka,*" they said. "It is useless to try and conquer such a man as Leppä. He laughs at our hardest labors. We shall have to give him our beautiful Katrina."

[184]

At last Katrina was brought. Her eyes were the color of the sea at midday. Her cheeks were like the rosy dawn, and her hair hung about her in ringlets of gold. When Leppä saw her, he knew she was so beautiful that her equal could not be found on land or sea.

Leppä thanked the King, took Katrina into the boat, and together with his companions set out from Kiijoki. Continuing their voyage, each companion left at the place on the shore where he had first met Leppä, until finally Leppä and Katrina were alone in the boat. As Leppä rowed, he noticed that the waves splashed Katrina's beautiful blue gown, and he lifted the folds with his forefinger from the water.

Leppä and Katrina found Loviatar waiting for them. She held out her skinny hand to Katrina, and bit off Leppä's forefinger.

"Since you touched the maiden with that finger," she screamed, "I have bitten it off."

This made Leppä hot with anger. He drew his sword as quick as lightning, struck the witch three strokes in the form of the cross, and so destroyed her.

When Katrina saw that Leppä had rescued her from the charm of the witch, she said:

"You are a brave man, and since you have saved me, I will gladly be your bride."

At these words Leppä was filled with joy. He ran to Loviatar's empty hut and took her gold and jewels. He mounted his horse, lifted Katrina before him on the saddle, and together they rode happily back to Leppä's own country.

But, alas, their joy was short! The King of Leppä's country and the Courtiers began to ask Leppä what had happened to his comrades, the three-bottle drinker and the six-bottle drinker, who had ridden out with him on his far journey. Leppä could not tell them, for if he did, he would be changed into a blue cross. And so he made up a strange story out of his brain, and expected the people to believe it.

But the people did not believe his story. Instead, they began to gossip and to imagine the worst. They all came to believe that Leppä had killed his faithful companions. When the King heard this, he gave a command to have Leppä put to death.

And so at last Leppä was forced to tell the truth. But as he came to tell how he had broken the spells of Loviatar by striking with his sword, he was changed instantly into a blue cross.

Katrina became the King's bride, for she was still the most beautiful woman in the world. And to this day travellers to that far northern land are still shown the blue cross that stands there upon a lonely hillside, a witness to the truth of Leppä's strange story.

LIISA AND THE PRINCE

There was once an old man, Māki, who lived in a *tupa* on the edge of the deep wild forest, with his wife and his small daughter, Liisa. He had a cow and a flock of sheep, and spent most of his time in the pastures.

One day when he was not watching, it chanced that his black lamb, Musti, strayed into the woods and was lost. Māki called his wife, and together they started to hunt for it, each going a different way through the trees.

The wife had gone but a short way when she met a spiteful Ogress in disguise.

"What is it you search for, my good woman?" asked the Ogress.

And when the wife looked up, the Ogress spat in her face and mumbled quickly:

"My body to you, yours to me."

[187]

The charm worked, and the wife became ugly and brown and wrinkled, while the Ogress looked exactly like Māki's wife, with yellow hair, and smooth skin, and rosy cheeks.

It was the Ogress who had hidden the black lamb, and now she ran and brought it to Māki, shouting:

"Māki, hoi! Hoi, ukko (Ho, Māki! Ho, old man) ! See, I have found our lost lamb!"

Māki took the Ogress for his own wife, and together they carried Musti home to the fold.

The real wife was left behind in the forest. She wandered about, weeping, for the Ogress had left her so dazed that she could not find her way home. Presently she came to a flock of sparrows chirping in a tree. She spoke to them, begging them to help her, but the birds only looked at her and flew away in terror.

At last she came to a brook. She stooped down beside it to quench her thirst, and there saw for the first time, how ugly her face had become. Then she knew she could never rejoin her family, for Māki would never believe that she was his wife.

She sat by the river bank under a birch tree for three days and nights, and wept. And at last her spirit left her and became the spirit of the tree.

Meantime the Ogress lived in the *tupa* with Māki and his pretty daughter, Liisa. After a year she had a daughter of her own whom she named Kirjo. This daughter at first was brown and wrinkled and ugly, but the Ogress by magic gave her a family resemblance to Liisa, so that it would seem she was her sister.

As soon as Kirjo was born, the Ogress hated Liisa and plagued her in every way to make her unhappy. She dressed her in ragged threadbare homespun, and made

[188]

her sleep alone in the *sauna*. During the day, poor Liisa did all the heavy work about the house, and at night she could do nothing but weep, for she knew that the Ogress was not her real mother.

As for Kirjo, the Ogress dressed her up in the finest linen, and set her beside Mäki at the table. At night she gave her the softest, warmest bed in the *tupa*.

Some years later the King gave a great feast at the castle. The young prince had just come of age, and his father wanted him to choose a bride. So he sent his soldiers out to gather all the people together. Into every village, along every highway the soldiers went singing:

Come all ye people far and wide,
Come high, come low, from every side,
Come rich, come poor, none are denied.

When the Ogress heard the invitation, she said to Mäki:

"Take Kirjo, and start on ahead. I'll give Liisa some work here at home, so she won't be lonesome while we are away, and then I will join you along the road."

The Ogress took Liisa into the bath house. She turned over the hearthstones, and scattered barley seeds everywhere on the floor and among the ashes.

"If you don't gather up every one of these seeds into this basket before I return from the castle," she said, "I will beat you every day as long as you live!"

Poor Liisa dried her tears when the Ogress had gone, and began to pick the barley seeds, one by one, from the ashes and from among the black hearth stones. After she had worked for hours, she saw that the task was hopeless. It was as if she had been set to pick the sand grains from the seashore. Tears blinded her eyes, and she decided to run away.

[189]

As Liisa was running through the forest, a great birch tree called after her:

"Liisa, Liisa, where do you run?"

Liisa stopped to see who was speaking.

"Do not be afraid," the tree continued. "I am the spirit of your mother. Dry your eyes and take one of my branches, and make a brush. With this sweep the hearth-stones, and the barley seeds will all fly into the basket as if by magic. When you have finished, bring the brush to me, and I will show you a great wonder."

Soon the barley seeds were all in the basket, and Liisa hurried back to the forest. Then her mother's spirit said:

"Bathe now in the river, and return to me and I will give you clothes such as you have never seen."

As Liisa came out of the water, she was transformed into the most beautiful woman in the kingdom. And then she returned to the birch tree. There she found a dress of the finest linen, and shoes of the softest white leather. Brilliant jewels glittered in her yellow hair, and rarest pearls were about her smooth white throat, and upon her slender fingers sparkled great diamonds. A prancing horse trapped in gold and silver stood waiting beside her. Liisa leapt to the saddle, and before she knew what was happening, the horse carried her to the garden beside the King's castle.

When the Prince Uvanto saw how beautiful Liisa was, he came running across the garden to meet her. He lifted her down from the saddle, tied her horse by the reins, and led her into the castle. Here he presented her to the King and the Court.

All the people of the countryside were assembled there, according to the King's order. When they saw Liisa they

[190]

began whispering. Everyone wondered who this beautiful stranger was and where she had come from, for not even Māki, her own father, knew her.

This made the Ogress very angry, for she was trying hard to catch the Prince's attention herself, so that he would ask Kirjo to sit beside him. But after a while he was so annoyed by their smirks and gestures that he ordered his guards to put the Ogress out of the room and to send Kirjo to sit in the stable with the servants, where she had only the left-over scraps to eat.

When the feast was over, and all the people were starting for their homes, Liisa asked the Prince if he would not help her to her horse.

"First you must give me some keepsake to remember you by," smiled the Prince, "for I hope to see you again very soon."

"Take this ring from my finger," said Liisa.

The Prince kissed her hand as he took the ring, and said to himself:

"It is a good thing you don't know how beautiful you really are."

The Prince led Liisa through the garden between the flowers and told her how he loved her. Then he lifted her to her saddle, and she rode off.

When Liisa reached the birch tree by the river, she left her fine horse and her clothes and her jewels, and told her mother's spirit all that had happened.

"One of the rings is lacking," she said, "because the Prince begged it as a remembrance."

"All is well," answered the mother's spirit. "Go back to the bath house, and don't worry."

Liisa did as her mother's spirit bade her, and when Māki and the Ogress and Kirjo arrived at the *tupa,* she pretended that she was just dropping the last barley seed into the basket. The Ogress was surprised to find the work finished, and she pretended to be sorry for Liisa.

"My poor Liisa," she said, "you have missed the feast at the King's castle, but such things are not for the like of you. My Kirjo, now, was quite at home. She had a wonderful time. Prince Uvanto asked her to sit beside him at the feast, and he kissed her hand, and invited her to come again."

Liisa knew this was not true, for she had seen all that had happened. Yet she said nothing, but did the hard work in silence, for the Ogress was now even more cruel.

As soon as Liisa had ridden away from the castle, the Prince looked at the sparkling diamond ring, and sighed for her return. If he had only known where she dwelt, he would have sent for her. And after a few weeks he felt so lonely that he begged the King to send his soldiers to search for Liisa.

"But the soldiers don't know who she is!" said the King.

"I have her ring," answered the Prince. "Take it and make a ring the same size for each of the soldiers to carry, and let them try the finger of every girl in the kingdom. In this way they can surely find the girl I love."

The rings were made, and the soldiers went out with them. One of the soldiers came to Mäki's *tupa* and said:

"It is the King's wish that each girl shall hold her finger out to see if the ring fits."

The Ogress by magic changed the size of Kirjo's finger so that the ring seemed to belong to it, but she hid Liisa behind her skirts so that the soldier did not notice her.

When the soldier saw how perfectly the ring fitted, he said to Kirjo:

[192]

"It is the King's wish that you come with me to the castle, for the Prince wishes to speak with you."

Kirjo gladly went with the soldier, and after they had gone, the Ogress turned sharply to Liisa.

"Dry your tears, you lazy girl! Stop dreaming, and get to work and finish scrubbing the floor. You were not meant for a Prince. The worst man alive would never marry you if he knew how lazy you were."

The next day Kirjo returned in tears:

"The Prince would have nothing to do with me," she complained. "There were forty other girls from every part of the realm. Our fingers all fitted the ring, but our faces did not please the Prince."

Now Liisa knew that the Prince was surely searching for her. Her heart leapt, but she held her tongue.

Five days later the King's soldiers were again sent out to call the people together. They went everywhere chanting:

> Come all ye people, far and wide,
> Come high, come low, from every side,
> Come rich, come poor, none be denied.

Again before she started with Māki and Kirjo to the King's castle, the Ogress took Liisa into the bath house. She kicked over the hearthstones, and scattered ashes about the floor, and then flung about a basket of the finest flax seed. As the seed flew everywhere, the Ogress said to Liisa:

"If every one of these flax seeds is not in the basket, and if the ashes are not in the hearth, and if the hearthstones are not in their places when I return from the castle, I will beat you with willow boughs morning and night as long as you live. Dry your tears, you lazy girl, and set to work."

As the Ogress left the bath house she slapped Liisa sharply across the cheek. Liisa tried to gather the flax seeds, but it was hopeless, for they were finer than needle points. Her eyes again filled with tears. And then she remembered her mother's spirit, and ran to the forest.

"Take another of my branches and make a broom," her mother's spirit whispered sweetly, "and sweep the flax seeds into the basket, the ashes into the hearth, and the hearth stones into place. When you have finished, return, and I will show you another wonder."

Soon Liisa was running back to the birch tree with a happy face, her work all done.

"Bathe again in the river," said her mother's spirit.

When Liisa came from the river this time, she was more beautiful than ever. The most gorgeous clothes awaited her, and when she was dressed, the same prancing steed in its gold and silver trappings stood before her. Liisa leapt into the saddle, and was soon at the King's castle.

The Prince was watching at the window, and when he caught the first glimpse of Liisa, he dashed across the garden to greet her.

"This time I will keep you, if I may," he said as he lifted her from her saddle.

Then he led Liisa into the castle and set her down beside him at the table.

Again all the people marvelled at her beauty. All tried to guess who she was, and where she came from. When the feast was finished and all the people were starting for their homes, the Prince tried to keep Liisa with him.

"Stay with me," he said, "and I will make you my princess."

[194]

"But you don't understand," replied Liisa. "I cannot stay today. Let me go, I pray you, for I must not be home late!"

"Then leave me something to remember you by," he pleaded.

"Here, then," said Liisa, "Take this earring."

After a few days the Prince was so sorry he had let Liisa go this second time that he begged the King to send out his soldiers to see if he could not find her.

"Father, tell your goldsmiths to make an earring for each of your soldiers like this one I have for a keepsake. When a woman is found who has the fellow to the earring, she will surely be the woman that I love."

This time when the soldiers came to Māki's *tupa*, the Ogress by magic made a fellow to the earring, and placed it in Kirjo's ear. The soldier was sure he had found the right woman, and carried Kirjo off to talk with the Prince.

Next day Kirjo returned again in tears.

"I was the only woman who had an earring to match," she said, "but the minute the Prince looked at me, he was angry, and sent me away."

Again Liisa's heart leapt within her, but she said nothing. The Ogress was so angry that she made Liisa work twice as hard.

When the soldiers failed to find the right woman, the earrings were thrown away, and the Prince begged the King to call all the people to another feast.

Again the King's soldiers went chanting throughout the land:

> Come all ye people, far and wide,
> Come high, come low, from every side,
> Come rich, come poor, none be denied.

This time before leaving for the castle with Māki and

Kirjo, the Ogress spilled a bowl of milk among the ashes and over the hearth stones, and said to Liisa:

"If you do not gather the milk into the bowl before I return you'll be sorry, for I will plague you day and night without mercy."

Her mother's spirit again helped Liisa, and when the milk was safely in the bowl to the last drop, she bathed, dressed, leapt upon the prancing steed, and was the third time carried to the King's castle.

The Prince Uvanto was waiting in the King's rose garden, and when Liisa arrived, he cried: "This time I shall keep you for my very own!"

And when the others were leaving, the Prince tried his best to keep Liisa by him.

"I cannot stay today," said Liisa. "A cruel Ogress is to blame for your not finding me."

"Then we must break the spiteful witch's charm," the Prince answered. "Leave me a keepsake so that I may search you out."

"Here is my slipper," answered Liisa.

The Prince looked at the dainty jewelled slipper, and sighed. He called together the wisest fortune tellers and magicians in the realm, and asked their advice. At last an old gypsy man tottered to the Prince's side and whispered:

"Come, Prince Uvanto, with me, and I will take you to the woman of your heart. You must bring twelve of your most trusted servants. Four shall carry tar and tinder, four shall carry fire, and four a blue carpet."

After a long winding journey, the old gypsy wise man, the Prince, and his twelve servants, came in sight of Mäki's *tupa*.

"O Prince," said the gypsy, "command your servants

[196]

to dig a pit before the door of the bath house. Fill it with tinder and tar, lay a platform of rotten wood over it, and spread on the platform the blue carpet. You and I will approach the *tupa,* and see what is happening."

The gypsy whispered a charm, and disguised himself and the Prince as two woodcutters. Through the window of the *tupa* they saw Liisa scrubbing the floor on her knees, while the Ogress scolded and Kirjo sat by on a silken cushion and sipped milk.

When the Ogress came to the door, the gypsy said:

"We found this strange jewelled slipper as we came near your *tupa.* Is there a girl here whose foot it fits?"

The Ogress examined the slipper, and by magic changed Kirjo's foot so that the slipper seemed exactly made for it. The Prince saw that this was the girl he had twice sent away from his castle, and Liisa felt her heart thump as she listened.

But the gypsy said:

"Good! The Prince would like you to go with your daughter to the castle, for he has something to say to her. But first you must take her to the bath house. There dress her in her finest linen, and make ready for the journey."

The Ogress did as she was bid, but when she and Kirjo stepped on the blue rug which the twelve servants had spread, the boards gave way, and they both fell into the burning tar, and were destroyed.

When Liisa saw all that was happening, she ran to the forest, bathed in the river, put on the gorgeous gown and the one jewelled slipper, and leapt upon the prancing steed. She heard the spirit of her mother saying:

"Now I shall rest in peace, for I know you are happy at last!"

The Prince Uvanto saw Liisa coming. He saw too that one of her tiny feet was bare. He placed the jewelled slipper which he had brought where it belonged, and off they rode to the castle. And now that the Ogress was dead, there they lived happily ever after.

II
DROLL STORIES

THE PIG-HEADED WIFE

When Matti married Liisa, he thought she was the pleasantest woman in the world. But it wasn't long before Liisa began to show her real character. Headstrong as a goat she was, and as fair set on having her own way.

Matti had been brought up to know that a husband should be the head of his family, so he tried to make his wife obey. But this didn't work with Liisa. It just made her all the more stubborn and pigheaded. Every time that Matti asked her to do one thing, she was bound to do the opposite, and work as he would she generally got her own way in the end.

Matti was a patient sort of man, and he put up with her ways as best he could, though his friends were ready enough to make fun of him for being henpecked. And so they managed to jog along fairly well.

But one year as harvest time came round, Matti thought to himself:

"Here am I, a jolly good-hearted fellow, that likes a bit of company. If only I had a pleasant sort of wife, now, it would be a fine thing to invite all our friends to the house, and have a nice dinner and drink and a good time. But it's no good thinking of it, for as sure as I propose a feast, Liisa will declare a fast."

And then a happy thought struck him.

"I'll see if I can't get the better of Liisa, all the same. I'll let on I want to be quiet, and then she'll be all for having the house full of guests." So a few days later he said:

"The harvest holidays will be here soon, but don't you go making any sweet cakes this year. We're too poor for that sort of thing."

"Poor! What are you talking about?" Liisa snapped. "We've never had more than we have this year. I'm certainly going to bake a cake, and a good big one, too."

"It works," thought Matti. "It works!" But all he said was:

"Well, if you make a cake, we won't need a pudding too. We mustn't be wasteful."

"Wasteful, indeed!" Liisa grumbled. "We shall have a pudding, and a big pudding!"

Matti pretended to sigh, and rolled his eyes.

"Pudding's bad enough, but if you take it in your head to serve stuffed pig again, we'll be ruined!"

"You'll kill our best pig," quoth Liisa, "and let's hear no more about it."

"But wine, Liisa," Matti went on. "Promise me you won't open a single bottle. We've barely enough to last us through the winter as it is."

Liisa stamped her foot.

"Are you crazy, man? Who ever heard of stuffed pig

without wine! We'll not only have wine, but I'll buy coffee too. I'll teach you to call me extravagant by the time I'm through with you!"

"Oh dear, oh dear," Matti sighed. "If you're going to invite a lot of guests, on top of everything else, that'll be the end of it. We can't possibly have guests."

"And have all the food spoil with no one to eat it, I suppose?" jeered Liisa. "Guests we'll have, and what's more, you'll sit at the head of the table, whether you like it or not."

"Well, at any rate I'll drink no wine myself," said Matti, growing bolder. "If I don't drink the others won't, and I tell you we'll need that wine to pull us through the winter."

Liisa turned on him, furious.

"You'll drink with your guests as a host should, till every bottle is empty. There! Now will you be quiet?"

When the day arrived, the guests came, and great was the feasting. They shouted and sang round the table, and Matti himself made more noise than any of his friends. So much so, that long before the feast was over Liisa began to suspect he had played a trick on her. It made her furious to see him so jolly and carefree.

As time went on she grew more and more contrary, until there was no living with her. Now, it happened one day in the spring when all the streams were high, that Matti and Liisa were crossing the wooden bridge over the little river which separated two of their meadows. Matti crossed first, and noticing that the boards were badly rotted, he called out without thinking:

"Look where you step, Liisa! The plank is rotten there. Go lightly or you'll break through."

"Step lightly!" shouted Liisa. "I'll do as . . ."

[203]

But for once Liisa didn't finish what she had to say. She jumped with all her weight on the rotted timbers, and fell plop into the swollen stream.

Matti scratched his head for a moment: then he started running upstream as fast as he could go.

Two fishermen along the bank saw him, and called: "What's the matter, my man? Why are you running upstream so fast?"

"My wife fell in the river," Matti panted, "and I'm afraid she's drowned."

"You're crazy," said the fishermen. "Anyone in his right mind would search downstream, not up!"

"Ah," said Matti, "but you don't know my Liisa! All her life she's been so pig-headed that even when she's dead she'd be bound to go against the current!"

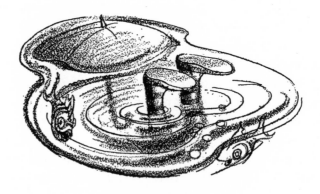

FINLAND'S GREATEST FISHERMAN

A fox was one day slinking along the edge of the deep, wild forest when he saw Ukko Rantala driving home in his sleigh with his catch of fish.

The fox was very hungry, and hunting was poor. He began to think how he could get some of the fish for himself.

"I'll lie down on the road," he said to himself, "and pretend to be dead. Then the fisherman will throw me into the back of the sleigh, and all will be well!"

It happened that old Rantala was very happy. He had taken a good catch of fish, and had also had a round of drinks with his friends. As he drove homeward, he sang, keeping time with the patter of the horse's hoofs:

"Hei, luulia, il-lala! Hui, luulia, il-la-la!" (A Finnish phrase similar to tra-la-la.)

Suddenly the horse stopped short, and snorted in fright.

Rantala looked about him, and there he saw the fox lying in the road. He climbed out, grabbed the limp fox by the tail, and threw it into the back of the sleigh beside his basket of fish.

"Am I not a lucky man today!" he laughed to himself as he whipped up his horse. "Not only plenty of fish, but a fine red fox! The wife will be pleased with me today! *Hei, luulia, il-la-la! Hei, luulia, il-la-la!*"

As soon as Rantala continued his singing, the fox opened his eyes and saw that he was safe. Rantala was much too happy to look behind him.

So the fox quietly lifted the fish out of the basket one at a time, and dropped them in the snow at the side of the road. As soon as the basket was empty, he leapt lightly from the sleigh, and gulped down the fish as fast as he could.

When Rantala reached home, he jumped from his sleigh, and began to unharness his horse, calling out loudly to his wife:

"*Tule Eukko,* come, wife, come welcome the greatest of Finland's fisherman and hunters! See what is in my sleigh!"

And as his wife came through the door, he laughed aloud with joy.

"A red fox is there," he shouted, "and the finest catch of fish a woman ever laid eyes on!"

But the wife could see nothing.

"*Ka,* drunk again!" she said with a sigh.

"There they are," Rantala insisted. "Look at what's lying by the basket! *Hei, luulia-li, il-la-la!*"

"*Ka,*" the wife cried in disgust. "Now we shall be hungry again!"

At last Rantala came to see what was the matter. He looked in the bottom of the sleigh, and in the bottom of the basket. He scratched his ear and thought, then said:

"It is not only that I am drunk. It is that the red fox was wiser than I."

STUPID PEIKKO

I

Peikko was a gnome who lived in the old days. He was very ugly, with a short, crooked body and bandy legs, like all gnomes, and he had a great idea of his own cleverness. He liked to spend his time with human beings and prided himself on being a great deal smarter than they were. But as a matter of fact he was really very stupid.

Among the young men in the village Peikko had one particular friend named Matti, whom he was always trying to outwit. One day he said to him:

"Listen, my friend, since you are so clever, make me a bridge across this brook here. But you must use neither wood nor stone nor iron."

Matti scratched his head and considered. The brook was very narrow. All at once he leaned over, braced his feet on one bank and his hands on the other.

"There's your bridge, Peikko," he laughed. "It is neither wood nor stone nor iron. Walk across and try it!"

Peikko was outdone that time, but the next time he thought he would surely get the better of Matti. There was to be a wedding in the village. Matti was always a great favorite with the girls at dancing, and Peikko who was a bit jealous of him thought it would be a grand trick to keep Matti from going to the wedding at all. So he said to him:

"Matti, I want you to do something for me this evening, and it's a job I wouldn't trust to everyone, either. I have a storehouse where I keep my sacks of gold. I don't dare leave it unwatched, but I have an important engagement tonight, so I want you to stand guard over my storehouse door while I'm away."

"I'll be glad to watch it for you," said Matti, "if you show me where it is."

"Come with me," said Peikko, and he led him to the building. "Now you stand guard, and be sure you don't leave the door once, while I go to the wedding."

"Wedding?" cried Matti. "Why didn't you tell me where you were going? I want to go to the wedding, too."

"I can't help that. You promised to guard my storehouse door, and mind you don't leave it one instant!"

"But I didn't know about the wedding."

All the same Matti had to sit down beside the door while Peikko pranced off to the wedding with a merry heart, thinking he'd got the better of Matti for once.

Matti thought and thought, and the more he thought the more he wanted to go to the wedding. After a while he had a bright idea. He pulled the door from its leather hinges, lifted it on his back and hurried off.

When he arrived he found the guests feasting gaily.

Peikko was there with the others, eating, drinking and shouting with laughter. When he looked up and saw Matti he was very surprised.

"Why Matti, what are you doing here?" he cried. "You've broken your promise. You swore you wouldn't leave that door for a single instant."

"Well, neither I have," said Matti. "I've brought it here on my back!"

Peikko stared at him. Then he lifted his glass.

"I drink your health, Matti," he said. "You're certainly smarter than I am."

II

It chanced another time that Matti had spent all his money. He knew that Peikko was very rich, like all gnomes, so he thought he would try to get some of that wealth for himself.

So he walked through the forest till he came to Peikko's hut, which was on the shore of a very pretty lake. There he sat himself down on the shore in front of the house and began to whistle softly. When he saw that Peikko had heard him and was coming, he leaned forward and began to drink the lake water in great gulps.

"You must be very thirsty," said Peikko, watching him. "Come into my *tupa* and I'll give you something better than water to drink."

"I'm not drinking the water because I'm thirsty," said Matti, "but because I want to drink the lake dry. It's like this, Peikko. Whenever I want to go anywhere, this lake is always in my way. I have no boat to cross it, so I have to walk around, and that's a nuisance. Besides, I'm always afraid someone will drown. So I've decided to drink the lake dry, and get rid of it once and for all."

As he spoke, Matti leaned down and began lapping the water again.

"Don't do that," cried Peikko. "I love this lake. I couldn't live without it. If you promise not to drink it dry I'll give you a bag of silver."

"Will you, indeed?" said Matti. "It'll need be a large bag to pay me for all the trouble I've been put to an account of this wretched lake of yours!"

"At least stop drinking till I go to my garden and fetch it!"

"I can't promise unless you hurry."

Foolish Peikko hobbled off to his garden as fast as his bandy legs would carry him, terrified lest Matti would drink the lake dry before he got back. But when he returned, the lake was still there, laughing in the sun.

And Matti laughed, too, as he hurried off with the bag of silver.

III

Some days after it happened that Peikko needed a man to help him roof his *tupa*. So he went to Matti, promising to fill his hat with silver as soon as the job was finished.

Matti agreed, and when the work was over he held his hat out and said:

"Your money is heavy, Peikko, and my hat is old and likely to tear. I'd better rest it on a stump while you fill it."

"Just as you like, Matti. While I fetch the silver, you find the stump."

Matti soon found a stump to his liking. It was old and rotten, and hollow to the root. Matti's hat too was old, and there was a hole in the crown which Peikko had not seen.

[210]

The addled old gnome hobbled on

Matti held the hat over the hole in the stump, and Peikko began to pour the money in.

"Your hat holds a lot," Peikko said as he began to empty the second bag.

The third bag just filled the hat to the brim. Peikko nodded as he looked at it.

"You are a wise man, Matti. It must be because your head is so large. Three sacks of silver it would hold. But I promise you I'll never bargain to fill your shirt."

"That's right," said Matti, trying to keep a straight face. "One of us has a hole in the side of his head and the other hasn't."

But this was too deep for stupid Peikko to understand. He could only shake his head as he walked away.

IV

Among other things Peikko was always bragging to Matti about his strength. By-and-by Matti grew tired of this, so to cure Peikko of boasting he proposed they have some contests.

First they went into the forest near Peikko's house to see which could fell the largest tree. Peikko wound his arms around the trunk of a tall white birch, and tugged and pushed until he was black in the face. But for all his tugging the tree stood firm and solid, and at last poor Peikko had to give it up.

It was Matti's turn. He too seized the birch in his arms. Then he shouted:

"It's giving, Peikko, it's giving! Stand out of the way!"

Peikko took to his heels and ran so that the tree would not fall on him. When he was out of sight Matti took his axe from the hollow stump where he had hidden it, and chopped the tree down in a couple of strokes. He called:

"Where are you, Peikko? It's quite safe now, the tree's down!"

Sure enough, when Peikko came back there lay the tree on the ground.

"Now we'll try our strength at lifting it," Matti said.

He seized one end of the tree and dragged it a few paces. Then Peikko lifted the end of the tree, too, but Matti, hidden by the leaves, set his foot on one of the trailing branches. Peikko puffed and tugged till he was tired, but the tree would not budge.

"You've won again," he grumbled.

"What shall we try next?" Mattie teased him.

"We'll try breaking a rock with our fingers. You won't beat me at that, for my fingers are stronger than yours."

"All right," said Matti, for he remembered that he had slipped a boiled potato into his pocket that morning for lunch.

Peikko found a white cobblestone, and Matti pretended to find one, too, and put it in his pocket. "You crush your stone first," he said.

Peikko took the cobble in his strong right hand and squeezed with all his might. Tears came to his eyes from the effort, but the stone didn't break.

"You needn't grin," he said peevishly to Matti. "You won't do any better yourself!"

"Watch me," Matti returned.

He drew out the boiled potato, set his teeth and pretended to squeeze very hard, while Peikko watched. Presently a few drops of water trickled from between his fingers. He took a long breath, then opened his fist and showed Peikko the crumbled pieces.

"That's strange," said Peikko. "It begins to look as if you were a wizard!"

[213]

"I'm no wizard," Matti laughed. "It's just that I'm stronger than you, though our stones were both the same size."

"How about throwing a stone?" said Peikko then. "I can throw farther than anyone I know."

As he spoke, he picked up a stone and hurled it very high into the air. It fell a long distance off, and Peikko smiled. "Try and beat that," he said.

Matti picked a stone up, balanced it a moment in his hand, then pretended to hurl it at the very instant that a bird darted past them up into the air.

"There, see that?" he shouted.

Peikko blinked in astonishment, for he had caught only a glimpse of something that flew through the air and out of sight into the clouds.

"You may be a wizard," he said, "but I don't believe you can throw my iron hammer further than I can."

Matti seized the hammer and swung it a few times as though to gauge its weight.

"Watch, Peikko. I'll throw it right into the sky. I'll make it lodge on top of that cloud over there."

"Then I won't be able to get it back again," Peikko cried.

"Of course you won't. Not unless the hammer should break the cloud and come down with the hailstones," said Matti very seriously. "But I don't think that's very likely to happen. At least, it never has happened with me yet."

"Stop! Don't throw it, Matti," Peikko begged, and he snatched the hammer from Matti's hand. "I'll believe you. I'm sure you are a wizard!"

"Wrong again, Peikko," Matti laughed. "I'm just stronger than you are, that's all. You have to give in!"

[214]

V

When the miller's daughter was married, the miller gave a grand wedding feast, and Peikko was invited. Peikko loved good food, and when they all sat down round the table he began to eat like a wolf. Meat, cakes and honey all began to disappear at a great rate, and all the other guests stared, for they had never seen a man so greedy. As the meal went on, the host began to worry for fear the food would not last out to the end. Yet Peikko ate and ate and ate.

At last the miller whispered to his wife: "We must get rid of Peikko, or there won't be a crumb for anyone else."

By this time the guests had begun to tell stories, seeing that Peikko gave them no chance at the food, and someone had spoken of snakes.

"The only thing in the world I'm afraid of is a snake. I can't bear to hear one hiss, even. Just the very thought of a snake makes me shiver!"

This gave the miller an idea. He ran for some green willow twigs, and threw them on the hot embers in the open fireplace. They burned slowly at first but soon burst into a blaze, and as they caught one by one the fresh sap in them began to hiss. "Ssss-sss-ss," they went as the flames swept them.

Peikko was emptying a great jug of mead down his throat when the sound caught his ear. He set the jug down in a great hurry.

"What's that noise?" he whispered.

"It's nothing," said Matti, who was sitting beside him. "Someone must have brought a snake into the house."

"I—I think I'd better go home," Peikko said as he pushed his chair back. "I don't feel very well."

Just then the hissing of the willow twigs grew louder.

"Yes, I must go—I must go at once," Peikko said, his teeth fairly chattering.

And without saying good-bye he jumped through the window and made off as fast as he could pelt, leaving the wedding feast to continue merrily without him.

VI

One day Peikko happened to meet a man with a handsome red beard. He turned to Matti, who was standing beside him, and said:

"How did that man get such a fine red beard?"

"Oh, that's easy," laughed Matti. "He just gilded it."

"I wish I had a red beard," said Peikko. "If I had, all the girls would fall in love with me."

"Come with me," said Matti, "and I'll see what can be done."

He prepared a great pot of tar, and when it was hot he told Peikko to dip his beard in it, and hold it there. Peikko did, and when the tar had cooled he tried to lift his head to see how fine his beard had become. But instead of turning color, his beard stuck fast in the tar, and he had to call for help.

Matti came and cut the beard off with a sharp knife, but it was months before Peikko dared to show his face again, for the story got around and all the girls in the village were laughing at him. After that he was quite content with his own black beard.

VII

As Peikko grew older, he grew more and more grasping. Often he took what did not belong to him. The miller, who was his nearest neighbor, began to miss things, and knew that Peikko must have stolen them. Tools, leather straps, everything, even his stock of grain began to dwindle.

One day Peikko came creeping to the miller's oat bin, and filled his cap and his pockets with oats. This time the miller saw him, but he said nothing. Instead, he made a pair of birch-bark shoes huge enough for a giant, and left them leaning against the wall of his *tupa*, in full view.

The next night when Peikko came to carry off more of the miller's grain, he saw the huge pair of shoes leaning there.

"*Ka,*" said Peikko to himself. "Whoever wears those shoes must be a giant. It'll be a pretty bad job for me if he catches me. I'd better be going!"

And without more ado he took to his heels and ran home as fast as he could.

VIII

In his old age Peikko began to grow childish. He became curious about little things, and often asked foolish questions. He was greedier than ever, too; he could let nothing alone.

One day he was walking with Matti when he saw a haystack in the field near by, and pointed at it with a foolish smile.

"What's that?"

"That's a reed from my mother's loom," Matti told him.

"Can I have it?"

"Certainly," Matti laughed.

With great effort Peikko managed to balance the hay-

cock on his back, and they walked on. Presently Peikko
saw an old boat rocking at anchor.

"What's that?"

"Oh, that's my mother's old shoe," said Matti.

"Can I have it?"

"Surely!"

With still more effort, Peikko balanced the boat on his
shoulder beside the hay.

A little later they passed a disused millstone, and
Peikko asked again with his foolish grin:

"What's that?"

"That's my mother's old spinning wheel," said Matti,
laughing till his sides shook.

"Can I have it?"

"Surely."

"But how can I carry it?" Peikko asked him.

"Tie it to a rope round your neck."

Peikko tied the millstone about his neck and hobbled
on as best he could.

At last they came to the edge of a lake.

"And what's that?" Peikko asked.

Matti was beginning to get tired of his foolish questions. He said: "*Ka,* it's a lake. What did you think
it was?"

"How can I get across?" Peikko asked.

"Use the boat you've got on your shoulder, stupid,"
cried Matti impatiently.

"A boat!" cried Peikko delightedly, for he had forgotten all about it. "A boat! So I have. I'll cross in the
boat. Won't you come with me, Matti?"

"I'll walk around," said Matti. "Your boat isn't strong
enough to hold two. And take care yourself, if you're
going to put all that load in it!"

[218]

But Peikko paid no heed to his warnings. The addled old gnome jumped into the boat before Matti could stop "*Hyvasti* (Good-bye)!" he piped.

When he reached the middle of the lake, the boat filled with water and sank. Some say that Peikko stood on the haycock and shouted for help and that his friends rescued him, and that he still lived to a ripe old age. Others say that he still dwells in the palace of the Water God at the bottom of the lake, and that there he has been restored to everlasting youth.

THE WISE MEN OF HOLMOLA

Years ago in a far-off corner of Finland, there was a
little town called Holmola. The people who lived there
were known as the *Holmolaiset*.

It was very seldom that a stranger ever went to Holmola. And from living year after year by themselves,
and never seeing or hearing anything of the outside
world, the people who lived there grew to be quite different from the rest of the people in Finland, and rather
queer in their ways. They were simple-minded and above
all cautious. They liked to turn everything over very
thoroughly in their minds before they came to any decision about it, and would make the most elaborate plans
about even the simplest details of their daily life. When
it came to any important question they would talk it
over for weeks and months and even years, before they
could make up their minds to act.

So in time the *Holmolaiset* grew to be quite a proverb among the other people of Finland, and the few strangers who visited them brought back some very funny stories about their ways.

I

When the folk at Holmola first began to grow rye, they had the greatest difficulty in the world deciding how to harvest it. In fact, while they sat around talking and arguing about how the job should be done, their first crop ripened and wasted. There were only a few handfuls saved to seed the ground for the second year.

By the time this second crop was ripe, the wise men of the village had thought out a very careful plan. Not a single grain was to be wasted this time. They divided the whole town into crews of seven men each, and each crew set solemnly to work.

The first man bent the rye stalks over, one at a time. The second man held a piece of wood under each stalk. The third man cut the stalk with a sharp hatchet. The fourth man gathered the stalks into sheaves, which the fifth man bound. The sixth man carried the sheaves away and the seventh built them into a stack. And all this took so long that most of their crop was lost again, for by working their hardest seven men together could only harvest two sheaves a day!

A stranger named Matti happened to visit the town while this great harvesting work was going on. He was so amused at all this elaborate system of theirs that he decided to teach them a thing or two. So he hurried back to his native town and returned with a sickle.

That night while the Holmola men were resting after their enormous labors, Matti went out by moonlight into

[221]

the rye field and in a very short time he cut and bound more sheaves than all the town folk together had been able to harvest in a week. Then he dropped his sickle beside the last sheaf he had bound, and went back to bed.

In the morning he came out to see what they would make of it all.

When the Holmola men found their rye all cut and bound, and the sickle lying on the ground beside it, they were struck dumb with surprise.

For a week and a day they did nothing but talk it over, and at last they decided that all this dangerous work must have been done by *noita keinojen,* or magic spells, and that the wizard who had done it had afterwards changed himself into the sickle. So now for their own safety they must get rid of the sickle, and the best way to do that would be to drown it.

They all agreed, after much discussion, that anyone who touched the sickle or came within an eel's length of it, would be taking his life in his hands. So they went to the woods and cut a long pole, then they tied a leather noose on the end of the pole, and with this they managed to drag the sickle along the ground.

All the town folk came out to watch. Sure enough, that sickle was alive! Didn't it fight every inch of the way, not to be drowned? It kept catching at roots and stumps and rocks, at the banks of ditches, and it was with the greatest trouble in the world that at last it was dragged to the edge of the lake.

And then? Then the wise men left it there, while they spent another day standing about and arguing as to how to get it into the water.

Finally they dragged it into a boat, and towed it out to the middle of the lake. With another pole and another

The sickle caught on the edge of the boat

noose they managed to tie a big rock to the sickle so that it wouldn't float. Then with a shout of triumph they tipped the rock into the water.

But not the sickle. The sickle caught on the edge of the boat, and now they were all in a panic. The wizard was struggling to the very last gasp. There he hung, clutching at their boat, trying to drown them. Sure enough the boat was tipping. The weight of the rock in the water was dragging it down, and in another minute there they all were, spluttering and paddling away for their lives.

But the sickle was drowned. It was safe at the bottom of the lake, and the whole town declared a month's holiday to celebrate their escape. Now they could go on in their own ways, as their fathers had done, with no fear of wizards coming to interfere with them.

When Matti went home and told his friends what had happened the news spread like wildfire, and all Finland was laughing.

II

When Matti next came to visit the *Holmolaiset,* he found them all in a great to-do, one arguing against the other. They had been arguing for over a year. And this is how it all began.

For as long as the oldest men of Holmola could remember, the *Holmolaiset* had always lived in *kotas,* or houses shaped like wigwams. Lately they had, after much thought, decided to build for themselves instead *tupas,* or simple one-room log huts.

They had planned the whole work very carefully, and divided their entire population into gangs. One man was to cut down the trees, another to trim the boughs, and four others would peel the bark off. The seventh man would measure the tree into lengths, while the eighth and ninth cut it up into logs. Then the next four would carry these logs to the spot where the *tupa* was to be built. The fourteenth and fifteenth would match the logs at the ends so that they fitted together, and the next four would set them in place for the walls. Later on others still would lay the roof.

The work went on slowly, but with no great difficulty. Nothing went wrong until the first *tupa* was completed.

Then a great shock awaited them.

The wise men of the village had reasoned that the special advantage of the *tupa* was that it would always be filled with sunshine, summer and winter alike. For they argued that by building the walls and laying the roof while the sun was shining, and carefully chinking all the cracks as they went along, the sunshine would be trapped inside the *tupa* and kept prisoner there forever.

But when their *tupas* came to be finished, instead of being filled with sunshine inside they were as black as pitch. And this so amazed the wise men after all their calculations, that they sat down to reason out just how it had happened.

They were all sure that the sunlight couldn't possibly have escaped of its own accord. Hadn't they walled it in and roofed it down with all the care in the world? No, someone had gone to work and let it out again; that was sure. And the only person that could possibly do this would have been a wizard. So they set about getting the sunlight back again by the use of charms and spells.

But the charms didn't work and the spells didn't work, so they all sat down in front of their *kotas* again to think out another plan. After months of arguing back and forth they came to an agreement. What they had to do was to carry the sunlight into each *tupa*. A very simple idea—why hadn't they thought of it sooner!

Again they organized the whole village. The women carded and spun and wove, and made great woolen sacks. When they were finished the men divided into groups. Eight men held each bag open to the sunlight. When it was filled, others closed the sack and bound it tightly before the sunlight could escape. Then the sacks were carried inside the *tupas*.

But no, this plan didn't seem to work, either. They tried it over and over again, but something seemed to happen to the sunlight each time. So down they sat themselves again to think it out, and the longer they argued the more they disagreed. What happened to the sunlight nobody could make out.

When Matti arrived, he found them all shouting and quarrelling sixteen to the dozen.

He listened to their careful arguments and their tales of woe, and then he said:

"Men of Holmola, I don't pretend to be wiser than anyone else. But in my town we have long ago discovered the secret of the sun. If you'll pay me a thousand marks I'll show you how to get the sunlight into your *tupas!*"

After a long pow-wow the villagers agreed.

"All right," said Matti. Now watch."

Into the nearest *tupa* he strode. He took his axe from his belt, hacked out a square hole in the wall, and in streamed the sunlight, flooding the earthern floor, the wooden benches and tables, with a golden glow.

The villagers were amazed. In fact they were so delighted with this great invention that they decided to improve upon it themselves. They started to hack the

[226]

whole wall down, shouting as they saw the sunshine pouring in more and more. They worked so hard that at last the whole roof came tumbling down on their heads.

And after this catastrophe they decided that, all things considered, a *kota* was a better kind of house for them than a *tupa*.

III

One cold winter day the *Holmolaiset* started out on their skiis to hunt bear.

Presently they came to a cave which looked promising. They could see by the tracks that there was a bear inside, but as usual they were in no hurry. They sat down outside the cave, ate their lunch, and began reasoning out the best thing to do. By the middle of the afternoon, they had decided to send Pekka, the strongest man in the village, into the cave on his hands and knees.

Pekka agreed to drag the bear out if the others would kill it. To make it safer for him, they tied a leather thong to his foot, so that if he needed help at any moment all he would have to do would be to kick his foot, and then they would drag him out of the cave before the bear could hurt him.

With great caution Pekka began crawling into the cave. But while he was crouched there on hands and knees, waiting for his eyes to become accustomed to the darkness, so that he could peer about him, up jumped the bear and bit off his head. Poor Pekka had only time to give one feeble kick with his foot.

Outside the cave the others were watching eagerly.

"*Ka,*" they said. "Now he's kicking his foot. The bear must be growling at him. Let's pull him out and see what has happened."

[227]

They dragged away, and out came Pekka. But he had no head! This was extraordinary. They began at once to argue about it.

"So! His head has disappeared!"

"How did that happen?" cried another.

"He surely had his head on when he crawled into the cave," said a third.

"No he didn't," insisted a fourth. "Pekka never had a head as long as I've known him."

"You're right. He must have been born headless. Some people are."

"What are you talking about," shouted another. "Of course Pekka had a head. I distinctly remember seeing his beard waggle when he was eating his pork just now. If he had a beard he must have had a head!"

The upshot was that by the time they had proved to everyone's satisfaction that Pekka really was dead, darkness had fallen, and they had to go home for the night and start their bear hunt all over again next morning.

IV

When Matti next visited Holmola, he was surprised to find nearly half the villagers missing. When he asked about it he was told this story.

It seemed that late in the autumn a fire had broken out in the brush around the lake shore, and had driven a pack of wolves from cover. The wolves got in among the village cattle that were grazing on the opposite shore, and killed the oldest cow. One of the herdsmen drove them off before they had time to eat the meat, and told the villagers what had happened.

The *Holmolaiset* rowed across the lake, discussing on their way what was the best thing to do. The cow was dead; there was no need for any lengthy arguments about that. But now that it was dead, what should be done about it? After many hours talk, they decided to roast the cow meat in front of the brush fire.

They brought the carcass back across the lake in their boats, but by this time the fire had nearly burned itself out. All the same, they cut their pieces of meat from the cow, and tried to roast them on sticks before the dying embers.

When they thought that the meat was cooked enough, and ought to be crisp and brown, they began to eat. But the meat didn't taste good at all; it was smoky and only half-cooked. So they threw it away and sat down to argue about what they should eat instead.

After some days they decided that it might be possible to catch some fish in the lake, and cook those to make a meal. Whereupon they got out their nets and dragged the lake, but not a fish could they find. So once more they sat down to talk it over.

Presently they all agreed that the best thing to eat would be porridge. But by this time, with all their talking and arguing, a hard frost had set in and the lake was covered with thick ice. They were very hungry and they had no kettle big enough to cook all the porridge they would want to eat, so they had the bright idea of preparing their porridge in the lake.

"We'll cut a big hole in the ice and pour our meal in," they decided, "and then we can all eat our fill."

After more discussion they finally agreed upon the exact size that the hole ought to be, and half a dozen men went out to mark the ice, while others followed with picks to cut out the hole.

Then the cook and his helpers marched out, and began

[229]

to pour the meal through the opening, stirring the water with a long stick. When they all decided that the porridge should by this time be thick enough to eat, the cook stooped down to taste it and make sure there was no mistake.

But it so happened that the cook slipped on the ice and went headlong through the hole.

The others waited for his return. As time went by and still he did not appear, they began to argue about why he stayed down there so long.

"The porridge is so good," said the oldest man, "that he must be sitting there on the bottom of the lake stuffing himself, eating up all our shares."

"That's so," cried the others. "There'll be none left for the rest of us!"

One of the villagers volunteered to find the cook and fetch him back. He went forward very cautiously, but he too slipped just at the wrong moment, as the cook had done, and went headlong through.

When neither of the two returned, the rest grew very indignant, and after some time a third man went to see what was happening down there. But as he leaned over the hole to shout he, too, slipped and down he went.

And so one by one, at intervals, they each went to find out what had happened to their companions, until the last man of all had tumbled through the hole.

And for all that Matti could learn, there they still were, sitting on the bottom of the lake, planning and arguing and eating their fill of porridge.

And there they may still be, to this very day.

PEKKA AND THE ROGUES

Pekka and his father lived in a little hut in the country. They had a small piece of land and a couple of cows. With this they managed well enough when the seasons were good, but there came a year when the crops failed, and they couldn't cut enough hay from their one meadow to feed both their cows through the winter. So the old man said: "Here we have two cows, and not enough to feed them. We had better sell one cow, and then we can buy hay to feed the other one."

So early one morning Pekka set off to market with the oldest cow, Kyllikki. Pekka had never been to town before, and as he neared the market place he walked slowly, staring at everything around him. Two young rogues, or "dog's teeth" as they say in Finland, saw him coming along, and thought they'd play a trick on him. So they shouted:

"Hello, hayseed! Where are you going with that goat?"

Pekka stared back at them, but said nothing. He knew they were making fun of him because his cow was so lean and thin.

The two rogues slipped round the corner, changed their caps and thrust their hands in their pockets, and called to him again:

"Hey, hayseed, how much will you take for that goat?"

Pekka stared again, but did not recognize them. He thought to himself: "This is our old Kyllikki all right, but why does everyone in town speak of her as a goat?"

Presently he saw the two rogues again, and this time they called: "Hark, my lad! Is that goat for sale?"

By this time Pekka was so mixed up in his mind he hardly knew what to answer. He stammered: "This isn't a goat. It's our old cow, Kyllikki."

"Nonsense," said the two strangers, "you must be crazy. Of course it's a goat, and a pretty poor goat at that."

At last poor Pekka was so confused that he let them have Kyllikki for the price of a goat. But as he watched them driving the old cow on towards the market, he began to come to his senses again. He knew he'd been cheated. He said to himself:

"I'll follow those two up and see what they do with Kyllikki."

Pekka stood among the crowd in the market place, and watched the two rogues sell his cow for a good price. It made him so angry he was determined to get his money back again.

So he went to the nearest inn, gave the innkeeper some coins and said:

"I'm going to fetch my two friends to have dinner here.

Pekka said nothing

When we are ready to leave I shall twirl my cap on my finger and ask you: 'Is everything paid for?' And you must answer, 'yes.' "

"Certainly I'll say 'yes.' Here's the money right in my hand."

Pekka went to two other inns, and made the same bargain at each. Then he hurried off in search of the two men who had cheated him. He said: "You gave me a good price for my goat, and now I want to stand treat. Come along and have dinner with me."

The rogues were surprised, but they thought Pekka must be even stupider than they had supposed, and so long as he had some money there might be a chance to get it back from him. So they slapped him on the back and went off with him arm in arm.

The three ate and drank and made merry, and when they were ready to leave Pekka stood up, twirled his cap on his finger and shouted to the innkeeper:

"Is everything paid for?"

"Certainly, sir," said the innkeeper, and bowed politely.

The two rogues looked at one another. They decided to keep close by Pekka, and see what would happen next. After strolling about for a while Pekka said: "Let's go into this inn here and see what their wine is like."

They followed him in cheerfully, and when they had emptied their glasses Pekka stood up again and twirled his cap.

"Is everything paid for?" he called to the innkeeper.

"Yes, sir! Glad to see you again, sir."

This time the two rogues couldn't control their curiosity any longer. They asked: "Why don't you pay for what you eat and drink the same as other people do?"

Pekka drawled in his country voice: "You see, it's like this. It's because of my cap. It doesn't look like much, but it's a magic cap. Years ago a wizard gave it to my father in payment for a service. All I need do is to twirl the cap on my finger and ask: "Is everything paid for?" And the answer is always 'yes.' "

"What will you take for that cap?" asked the rogues, very excited.

"Take for it? I wouldn't dream of selling it," said Pekka. "I earn my living by it, as you can see."

"But we'll give you a good price."

"I'd rather keep the cap."

By this time they had come to another inn, and Pekka said: "Come on, and we'll have another bottle of wine in here. You'll see that it always works."

They entered the third inn, and everything happened as before. They drank their bottle, Pekka twirled his cap, and the innkeeper bowed and smiled.

When they were in the street again the rogues were determined to get that cap, pay what they might.

"We'll give you all our money," they promised.

Pekka scratched his head.

"How about that gold watch you've got?"

"You can have the watch, too."

"But then I'd have no cap to wear."

"Take either of our caps, whichever you like."

Pekka chose the best cap, tried it on, and finally agreed to the bargain. Then he took the money and the watch, and lost no time in getting out of town. After which he made for home as fast as he could.

Meanwhile the two rogues went to the best inn in the town, ordered an expensive dinner and plenty of wine, and when they had finished they twirled the shabby old cap directly in front of the innkeeper's eyes and asked:

"Is everything paid for?"

"Of course it isn't," cried the innkeeper.

"What do you mean?" cried the rogues. They twirled the cap again, and shouted: "Is everything paid for?"

"Are you crazy," cried the innkeeper, out of all patience, "or do you think you can make a fool of me? I'll soon show you!"

And he fell upon the two and beat them unmercifully.

When Pekka reached home he rushed breathless into the hut and laid down the watch, the money and his fine fur cap on the table. "What do you think of that?" he asked his father.

"But you never got all that for our old Kyllikki?"

Pekka grinned.

"No," he said. "You see, I sold my cap as well!"

III
FABLES

THE END OF THE WORLD

The little brown hen was out walking in the wood. Presently an acorn fell on her head.

"Goodness, what a crash!" cried the hen. "The sky is falling to pieces. Yes, that is what hit me! The world is coming to an end!"

And off she rushed, squawking. Presently she met the pig.

"Hurry, hurry," she screamed. "The world is coming to an end. A big piece of sky fell down and hit me. Let's run, quick."

"Oh dear," squealed the pig, and he began to run, too. "We must warn all our friends."

When the cow, the dog and the rooster heard what was happening, they all began to scream and run. "The world is coming to an end! What shall we do?"

They made such a noise that the fox, the wolf and the bear heard them shouting, and came running to see.

"Where are you rushing to?" the bear asked. "What is happening?"

"Haven't you heard?" chattered the hen. "The world is coming to an end. We are going to hide in the forest. Hurry, if you want to save your lives!"

"Heavens!" cried the wolf, the fox and the bear, and they all began running.

At last they came to a hollow in the forest, hidden by tall trees.

"Here is a good place to hide," said the hen.

And here they all hid. They waited and they waited, but nothing happened, and by-and-by they all began to feel very hungry.

"What shall we eat?" they asked one another.

The fox looked around, and saw the hen.

"Ka," he said, licking his chops. "It was the hen that started all this foolishness. We'll eat the hen first."

And before the hen could say a single word they all fell on her and gobbled her up.

But they were still hungry.

"We'll eat the pig next," cried the fox, "because he's so stupid he believed every word the hen told him."

So they ate the pig, too. By this time all the other barnyard animals were too frightened to move, and one by one the fox, the wolf and the bear ate them all up in turn, first the rooster, then the dog and then the cow.

"This has been a very pleasant excursion," said the fox.

"I feel as full as a tick," the bear grinned.

"I've eaten so much I must lie down and sleep," said the wolf.

They all curled up and slept, but when they woke up they were as hungry as ever.

"What shall we eat now?" asked the bear and the wolf, and they both looked at the fox, because he was the smallest.

"I," said the fox, "am going to eat myself."

And he turned his head and pretended to gnaw at his own tail.

The bear and the wolf thought that was a good idea, so they began to do the same. But while they were busy gnawing away the fox jumped out of the hollow and shouted:

"You are fools to eat yourselves up, but I'd be crazier still if I stayed with you!"

And off he galloped through the forest.

THE ROOSTER AND THE HEN

One day a hen and a rooster went into the *sauna* to take a bath. The rooster said:

"Hen, fetch me some water from the well. There isn't enough in the bucket here to wet the stones."

The hen went to the well and said:

"Good well, kind well, give me some water."

"I'll give you water if you fetch me a dipper," said the well. So the hen went to the woman of the house.

"Good lady, kind lady, give me a dipper."

"I'll give you a dipper if you'll fetch me a pair of shoes," said the woman. So the hen went to the shoemaker and said:

"Good shoemaker, kind shoemaker, give me a pair of shoes."

"I'll give you the shoes if you'll fetch me an awl," said the shoemaker. So the hen went to the blacksmith and said:

"Good blacksmith, kind blacksmith, give me an awl."

"I'll give you an awl if you'll fetch me some iron," said the blacksmith.

The hen went to the marsh, and said: "Good marsh, kind marsh, give me some iron."

And the marsh was a good and kind marsh, and it gave the hen some iron.

The hen took the iron to the blacksmith, and got the awl.

She took the awl to the shoemaker and got the shoes.

She took the shoes to the woman, and got the dipper.

She took the dipper to the well, and got the water.

But alas, when the hen hurried to the *sauna* with the water, she found the poor rooster dead from heat!

THE MOUSE THAT TURNED TAILOR

Once a cat caught a mouse, and began playing with it. The mouse begged:

"Please, Mr. Cat, don't eat me up, and I'll do anything you ask."

"Will you make me a suit of clothes, if I let you live?" asked the cat, still holding the mouse between his paws.

"I'll make anything you like."

The cat brought a piece of leather, and said: "Make me a coat out of that. But when you've finished the coat, I shall eat you."

When the cat came back for his coat, the mouse said:

"I'm sorry. There's wasn't enough leather to make a coat."

"Well, what can you make, then?" snarled the cat.

"I can make you trousers."

"All right," said the cat, "but when you've finished the trousers I shall eat you up."

When he came back for the trousers, the mouse said:

"I'm terribly sorry, but there wasn't enough leather to make a pair of cat's trousers."

"Then what can you make?"

"I can make you a vest."

"Then hurry up about it," snapped the cat, "and when the vest is done I shall eat you up."

Next day the cat came for his vest, but there were tears in the mouse's eyes.

"I'm so sorry, but the leather was too small for your vest."

"I've had about enough of this nonsense," growled the cat. "Tell me once and for all what you can make, and be quick about it, or I'll eat you up."

"I might make you a cap."

When the mouse saw the cat coming next time, he began to weep.

"The leather wouldn't even make you a cap."

"This has gone far enough," said the cat. "What *will* the leather make?"

"Gloves," said the mouse meekly.

But when the cat returned for the gloves the mouse said:

"The leather seems smaller and smaller. There's just enough to make you a purse to keep your money in."

"Then be quick about it," said the cat. "This is your last chance. Next time I shall eat you up, whether the purse is finished or not."

But when he came back for his purse next day, he found a notice to say that his tailor had left for China, to make coats and trousers and vests and caps and gloves and pocketbooks for the Chinese cats.

THE FEAST

For a long time the wolf and the bear had wanted to have a feast all by themselves, without being bothered by any of the other forest animals. So they killed three cows, and made ready to have a good time all alone.

But the sparrow, who is a great busybody, found out what was going on, and the fox happened to hear the sparrow gossiping about it to his mate.

The fox was very angry because he had not been invited, so he made up his mind to go to the feast whether or no. He went to the wildcat and said:

"The wolf and the bear are to have a great feast. Don't you want to come?"

"Of course I'll come," screeched the wildcat.

"Then you must do what I tell you," said the fox.

The fox went to call on the wolf and the bear, and said: "I should like very much to come to your feast, if it wasn't for my friend. I feel I ought to bring him, too, but I don't dare to because he has such ferocious manners."

This made the wolf and the bear very curious, just as the fox had hoped. They began to prick up their ears at once.

"Who is your friend?" they asked. "What does he look like?"

"He is neither very large, nor very small," answered the fox. "He has long whiskers, a long tail, and the most terrible voice in the world. If you once heard him speak you would be scared to death."

"Bring him along," cried the wolf and the bear. "We never heard of such a creature and we'd like to see him. To be sure, he can't frighten us!"

When the day came the bear and the wolf had everything all prepared. They set out the feast, and waited for the fox and his strange friend.

Presently they heard a little rustle in the bushes, and the sound of a light footfall.

"Here they come," said the wolf, winking at the bear.

The bear began to laugh. "This is going to be fun," he said. "The idea of the fox thinking he can frighten us!"

"The creature can't be very large," said the wolf, "for I can see nothing of him as yet."

All at once there came a horrible screech from the bushes. It sounded like nothing that the wolf or the bear had ever heard before. The bear began to shiver. Next instant the wildcat leapt out, his hair all on end and his yellow eyes blazing. The bear ran to climb a birch tree, with the wolf at his heels. But the wildcat sprang right on top of them, and down they all rolled together.

When the wolf and the bear could pick themselves up again they ran pell-mell to their caves, thankful to escape and without looking once behind them.

Then the wily fox crept out from his hiding place, and he and the wildcat laughed long and loud over their feast.

FARMERS THREE

Once a fox, a wolf and a bear decided to become farmers.

"We will till the fields just as the men do," said the fox.

So they planned to cut down trees, burn brush, plow the ground, sow seed and reap the grain.

But when it came to felling the trees, the wolf and the bear found that they had chosen a very hard task. The fox slipped away, and only peeped out once in a while to see how they were getting on. He was no help at all. The bear could only wrestle with the stumps and drag boulders from the ground. So it fell to the wolf to hold the axe between his paws, as best he could.

When the trees were finally cut, the fox came back to say he was very sorry he had been too busy to help. He'd do better next time, he assured them.

But when it came time to burn the brush, the fox said: "I'm sorry, but I shall have to leave you again. The smoke makes me so dizzy I can't see anything."

The bear and the wolf went on working. The bear fell in the hot ashes and singed his fur and blistered his paws, and the wolf's eyes smarted so from the smoke that tears ran down his cheeks.

After the brush was burned, there was all the plowing to do. The bear was the horse, and pulled the plow till his shoulders ached, while the wolf's paws were sore from holding the plow handle. By the time the field was all harrowed and the seed sown, the wolf and the bear were completely worn out.

When harvest time came, back came the fox.

"Now I'll make up for lost time," he told the others. "I'll do my share of the work, and more. I'll gather all the grain while you thrash it."

So again the wolf blistered his paws wielding the flail, while the bear was nearly blinded by the dust and the flying chaff. All that the fox had to do was to bite the stalks with his sharp teeth.

"Now our harvest is gathered," said the fox when the threshing was all over, "I suggest that we divide the crop according to our sizes. The bear is the largest, so he must have the largest share. You, wolf, come next, so you shall have the next largest. I am the smallest, so I'll be content with the least."

"Agreed, agreed!" cried the two others, for they thought the fox was being very generous. And they let him make the division.

The straw was by far the largest part of the harvest, so he gave that to the bear. The wolf got the chaff, for that was the next largest heap. And the smallest pile of all, the ripe yellow kernels of grain, the clever fox kept for himself.

WHY THE SQUIRREL LIVES IN TREES

The wolf and the dog used to be close friends. But one day they had a quarrel, because each thought that he was the stronger. The wolf said:

"The only way to settle the question is to have a battle. You gather all the barnyard animals on your side, and I'll gather all the forest animals."

"Agreed," said the dog.

So the dog called the cow, the pig, the sheep and the cat on his side, and the wolf brought the bear, the fox, the rabbit and the squirrel.

As the two armies drew near one another, the dog whispered to the cat: "Crouch low, creep up to the bear, and when no one is looking catch him by the throat and cling on as tight as you can."

The cat did so, and the bear was taken quite by surprise. He tumbled over on his back, shouting:

"Help, help! Someone is clutching my throat!"

When the other animals saw their biggest cousin on his back calling for help they were all terrified, and fled back to the forest, so the dog won the battle. But the squirrel was too small to run with the others, so he jumped into a tree, clapped his paws together and shouted:

"Wonders have come to pass! The smallest animal of the barnyard has conquered the biggest animal of the forest! It's no longer safe to live on the earth where such strange things happen!"

And to this very day the squirrel has continued to live in the tree tops, where he can sit in safety and mock the creatures that live on the earth.

THE VAIN BEAR

The bear was not always vain. There was a time when he paid very little attention to his looks. One day, however, he happened to notice what a beautiful red coat the fox had, and he grew very envious. He asked the fox:

"Cousin, where did you get such a beautiful red coat?"

"My coat?" said the fox. "Why, I climbed on a hay stack one day, and my friends set fire to the hay underneath me. I let my coat burn a little, and ever since it has been this beautiful color that you see."

"Really?" said the bear. "I wish you'd do the same for me. I'd like to have a red coat, too."

"Gladly," said the fox, laughing to himself. "There is a hay stack over in that field. Climb up on it and I'll light the fire."

The bear clambered up to the top of the stack, shouting: "Hurry, cousin, hurry!"

So the fox set fire to the hay, and soon the bear was nearly smothered in smoke.

"It's burning," he cried. "It's burning! Shall I jump down?"

"It's not ready yet, wait a little longer!" the fox called back.

Just then a wind sprang up and the hay burst into flame. The bear's long fur caught fire and he jumped from the hay stack and dived into the stream.

"Wait till I catch you!" he called to the fox. But the fox had already run away.

And ever since that day the bear's fur has been dark and coarse, and singed at the tips.

THE STUPID WOLF

A wolf was wandering through the forest one day when he came across a sow with her litter of little pink pigs.

"A-ha," said the wolf to himself. "Now I'll have a fine meal."

So he went up to the sow and said: "Listen to me. I'm going to eat up your young pigs."

"Please don't eat them just yet," begged the sow. "Do let me baptise them first. They haven't been christened yet."

"All right," said the wolf. "I'll give you exactly five minutes."

He sat down on the river bank to wait. The old sow called her litter together and led them down to the water's edge. Then she pushed them all into the water and swam with them quickly to the opposite shore.

When he saw what she was doing, the wolf shrugged his shoulders and said: "Never mind. Next time I'll be wiser!"

So he went on his way, and presently he came to a hillside where two rams were busy fighting. He shouted: "Stop your fighting, for I'm going to eat you up!"

"Don't eat us till we've settled our quarrel," cried the rams. "If you eat us now we'll go on fighting inside you and upset your stomach."

"All right," said the wolf. "Go on with your fight, and I'll wait till it's settled."

The rams wasted no time. Still butting and prancing, they edged further and further away from him, whereupon they took to their heels and ran till they reached the door of the farmer's *tupa*.

As the wolf went on his way he muttered: "I begin to think I'm a fool, but next time I'll know better."

He was nearly famished when at last he caught sight of two goats in the pasture. "There's a good meal at last," he said as he galloped towards them.

"I have come to eat you!" he shouted.

"Not yet, not yet," cried the goats. "Give us time to sing one parting song."

"All right," said the wolf. "I like music. I'll let you sing one song, and then I'll eat you up."

The goats lifted their heads, and let forth a great cry. Some men in a nearby field heard them and came running, and the wolf had to flee for his life.

As he reached the forest, out of breath and almost starving, he said to himself:

"What a fool they have all made of me! Was I a vicar that I must watch the sow's litter being baptised? Was I judge that I must settle the quarrel of the rams? Was I a musician that I must hear the goats sing? Alas, why was I born so stupid!"

[252]

THE WISDOM OF THE RABBIT

One day the rabbit was feeling particularly pleased with himself. He thought he was the finest fellow alive and could match his wits with anyone. He was prancing along, flapping his ears and twitching his whiskers, when he met a fox.

"Good morning, Mr. Fox," said the rabbit. "How would you like to have a bet with me?"

"I'd be delighted," said the fox, "especially to make a bet with you."

"*Ka*," said the rabbit. "You flatter me. However, let's mark a straight line on the ground. Whoever jumps over the line first shall win half the other's possessions."

"Fine," said the fox. "Are you ready to begin?"

"Not yet," answered the rabbit. "I want to think a moment first."

"Think as long as you like, my friend," said the fox gaily, "if you hope that thinking will mend your wits."

"I am thinking," answered the rabbit.

Just then a crow flew past and the fox turned his head to see where he was going. While the fox was looking the other way the rabbit shouted suddenly: "I'm ready!"

And before the fox could turn around, he had jumped over the line.

THE FOX AND THE RABBIT

A fox once met a rabbit in the woods, and began teasing him.

"You think you're a fine fellow, Mr. Bunny, but for all your airs no one is afraid of you. You couldn't even scare the biggest coward alive!"

"Is that so?" returned the rabbit angrily. "If you want to know, I'm as brave as anybody, and lots of people are afraid of me, too."

"*Ka,*" bragged the fox. "I don't believe you. Everyone is afraid of me!"

"I'll wager that I can frighten creatures a dozen times bigger than I am."

"Agreed," said the fox. "If you scare anyone bigger than a grasshopper, I'll miss my guess!"

The wager was laid, and the fox and the rabbit set off along the road. Presently they came to a field where some sheep were grazing. The rabbit hopped on the fence, and from the fence jumped down right into the middle of the flock. The sheep, taken by surprise, began running this way and that, bleating loudly.

The rabbit slipped back into the road again, and when he had recovered from his own fright he said:

"You see, Mr. Fox, I'm not such a coward as you thought. Didn't I set all those big sheep running!"

And so the rabbit won his bet, and again the fox was defeated.

THE WILY FOX

A fox one day passed a tree where a mother crow had built her nest. He circled about, peering up at all the nearby trees in turn, then he came back and looked at the crow's nest.

After a while the mother crow grew uneasy, and called down to him:

"What are you staring up here for?"

"I am going to make me a ski-pole. It seems that you've built your nest in the only tree that suits me, so I'm afraid I'll have to cut the tree down."

"Oh, you mustn't do that," wailed the crow. "My children are not old enough to fly, and they'll all be killed!"

"*Vai niin* (Is that so)?" said the fox. "Very well, I'll take pity on you, then. If you'll throw me down one of your fledglings for my dinner I'll see if I can't find myself another tree."

"It must be as you say," wept the crow, thinking to save the rest of her children at least.

The fox ate up the young crow that the mother threw down to him and went away licking his chops.

Next day he came back and said to the crow: "It's too bad. I've searched everywhere, but this is the only tree that will make me a good ski-pole."

Again the crow began to weep and wail.

"Very well," said the fox, "give me another young crow, and I'll find another tree."

So the crow had to give the fox another fledgling, and he went away smiling from ear to ear.

On the third day he came back again, and the same thing happened.

Soon after a hawk flew past, and said: "You poor mother crow, why are you weeping like that?"

"A fox comes every day and threatens to cut down my tree. I've already given him three of my children, but he's never satisfied."

"The fox is tricking you," answered the hawk. "When he comes again, ask him how he expects to cut your tree down without an axe."

The next day when the fox returned, the crow began to taunt him.

"Long tail, bushy tail, how can you cut down my tree? The hawk says you couldn't use an axe even if you had one."

"Is that so?" snarled the fox. "Just you wait till I've finished with your friend the hawk!"

And off he went, planning revenge. He stretched himself out on a hillside and pretended to be dead. After a time the hawk saw him, and began circling curiously about. The fox let his tongue hang out, lying there so stiff and still that the hawk was completely fooled. He alighted beside the fox and began pecking at his tongue.

But at this the fox gave a sudden snap with his jaws, and that was the end of all the hawk's wise counsel.

That day the fox had a fine dinner, and as he licked his lips he said to himself: "Even those who give the best advice are sometimes stupid."

THE STUPID BEAR

One day the bear caught a live seagull in his mouth, and was carrying it home for dinner when he met a fox.

"Hullo, cousin," said the fox. "From what quarter is the wind blowing today?"

The fox hoped that the bear would open his mouth and let go of the seagull, but the bear knew that the fox was always up to tricks, so he kept his mouth shut and said nothing. He just stared stupidly up at the sky.

Then the fox said:

"Cousin, I don't believe you are wise enough to answer this question. From what quarter does the wind blow when the midday sun shines in your eyes, but you feel the wind on your back?"

"From the north," answered the bear at once, for if there was one thing he was proud of, it was his wood lore.

But when he opened his mouth to speak the gull fell from his teeth, and before he knew what had happened the fox had snatched it up and sped off into the woods.

"That is what I get for my stupidity," said the bear as he shambled sadly away.

THE SONG OF THE FOX

It was some time after this that the fox stole some milk from the farmer's wife. He had lapped it up so eagerly that he splashed the cream all over his face. As he was going home through the forest the bear met him, took one look at his white-smeared face, and cried:

"Whatever has happened to you, that you look like that?"

The fox put on a pitiful look, drooped his head, and answered:

"Cousin, I met with a great misfortune. I was walking along quietly through the field by the farmer's house when the farmer's wife saw me, ran after me and beat me with a stick. Just look what she did to my face!"

The bear forgot all the fox's trickiness, and exclaimed: "My poor friend, you certainly have been ill-treated! What a shame! Climb on my back and I'll carry you anywhere you want to go. I'm sure it must hurt you to walk."

The fox climbed on the bear's back and rode there very comfortably. After they had gone a little way he couldn't resist teasing the bear a bit, so he began to hum a little song to himself.

"Hm . . . hm . . . hm. It's a funny world. Everything is topsy-turvy. The sick carry the well and the idiot carries the wise man."

For a while the bear paid no attention. But all at once he growled: "What's that you are singing away there?"

"Nothing," said the fox. "Nothing at all. I only said that the strong carry the weak, and he who has not been beaten carries the beaten one."

"You didn't sing anything of the kind," shouted the bear. "You sang just the opposite. And if you open your mouth again I'll teach you a new kind of a song!"

"I sing nothing at all, Honey Paw," replied the fox meekly.

But before they had gone very far he began again.

"The sick carry the well, and the—"

But this time he didn't finish, for the bear suddenly turned his head and shook the fox off his back, flop into the ditch.

"That'll give you something to sing about," he grumbled as he hurried off into the forest, leaving the fox to pick himself up as best he might.

THE SONG OF THE WOLF

A wolf once met a dog and said to him:

"Brother, won't you help me find some food? I am very hungry."

"*Ka*, surely I will. There is a wedding in the house near the marsh, and while everyone is making merry we'll manage to slip in. But if I take you along, you must promise to be very quiet!" answered the dog.

"I'll be quiet," answered the wolf. "You can trust me."

"Come along then," said the dog.

So he led the wolf into the house without anyone noticing, and they slipped under the table.

The guests threw scraps of meat to the dog, for they thought he was alone. The dog shared these with the wolf until they had both eaten their fill.

The wolf, however, was so greedy that he was not even satisfied with what he got. When one of the guests placed a bowl of mead on the floor, he darted toward it, lapping it up before anyone noticed him.

The mead made the wolf light-headed, and he wanted to sing, for he thought he had a fine voice.

The dog growled at him:

"Remember your promise to keep still."

"There's no danger," replied the wolf with a silly grin. "The other guests are singing. I want to join in!"

"You'd better take care," warned the dog.

But the wolf paid no attention. He lifted his nose toward the rafters, and howled in his loudest voice.

"Isn't it a pity that no one notices my wonderful voice," he sadly said to the dog.

But he had scarcely finished speaking before the men seized their staves and beat him so unmercifully that his back has been stiff ever since.

THE WOLF AND THE FOX

It happened once upon a time that a wolf and a fox were racing together through the forest when they fell into a deep pit. Each blamed the other for his mishap, and each began secretly planning how to escape.

At last on the third day the fox hit upon a plan.

"Listen, cousin," said he to the wolf. "I believe the sun is rising. You are taller than I. Won't you please stand on your hind feet against the wall of the pit, and try if you can see out?"

The wolf saw no harm in this, and did as the fox suggested.

Then the sly fox leapt upon the wolf's shoulders, and jumped over the edge of the pit to freedom.

When the wolf saw what had happened, he called:

"Cousin, since you have a good view up there, sit down here on the edge of the pit, and tell me where the sun really is rising."

The wolf's words sounded so simple that the fox turned around, and his long bushy tail trailed over the side of the pit.

The wolf grabbed the fox's tail, and dragged him back into the pit again.

"I was so lonely here that you can't blame me," said the wolf.

"Let's patch up our quarrel," answered the fox, "and see if we can't help each other out of this trap."

"Agreed," said the wolf.

So they sat down to think out a way to free themselves. After a long time the fox said:

"This pit was surely dug by man to catch the animals of the forest. Before long the man who made it will come to see if anyone has fallen into his trap. When we hear his footsteps we'll both lie down flat and pretend to be dead. When the man gets into the pit, he'll throw me out first, because I'm the smallest. Then I'll jump to my feet, and while's he's still gaping to see what happened you can climb on his shoulders and jump out, too, and then we'll both escape together."

The fox had barely finished speaking before the man came by, and everything happened just as he had said.

And so from that day on the wolf has always felt kindly towards the fox for saving his life, and though the fox still plays tricks upon him now and then, he is still grateful.

THE BEAR GOES FISHING

One day the bear was prowling through the forest when he came upon the fox, enjoying a meal of fish that he had stolen from the farmer.

"Hello, brother," cried the bear. "Where did you get that fine fish?"

The fox wiped his mouth with his paw.

"Where?" he said. "Why, I fished for that fish in the lake, of course."

"Can I get some too?" the bear asked.

"Surely," said the fox. "Just go to the lake and hang your tail down through the ice. When the fish bite at your tail, all you need do is to jerk them out quickly from the water."

The bear did as he was told. He dropped his long shaggy tail through a hole in the ice, and sat there waiting. He sat for a very long time, until night came, but he caught no fish. By-and-by his tail froze fast into the ice.

At last the bear grew tired; he thought he would go home. When he tried to get up, his tail was held fast. He pulled and he jerked and he jerked and he pulled, and at last his tail snapped off short.

And that is why the bear has no tail, to this very day.

THE FOX AS A JUDGE

Once upon a time a bear discovered a fresh bin of oats, and began regularly to visit it. The farmer discovered his tracks, and saw that the oats were rapidly disappearing. So he set a trap, and luckily caught the bear the very next day.

As soon as the bear felt the trap close upon his paw, he began to cry with pain, and to twist about with all his might to free himself. At length after much suffering, he managed to squeeze out of the trap. Then he started toward the farmer's house.

"I will eat that farmer alive," growled the bear furiously as he hobbled along.

The farmer happened to be chopping wood when the bear arrived.

"I'll settle with you for trying to catch me in your trap," snarled the bear. "I am going to eat you alive."

"Please don't do that!" said the farmer. "At least wait until we have settled who is to blame! You began the trouble by eating my oats, you know. Let's find a judge and put our case before him, and we'll abide by his decision."

"Agreed," growled the bear, and together they set out through the forest to find a judge.

They met a fox, and told him what had happened between them.

"Will you be the judge, and settle our dispute?" they asked.

"That I will," answered the fox, "but first we must go to the place where all this happened."

When they came to the oat bin, the fox said to the bear:

"Is this where you stole the oats?"

"Yes," grumbled the bear.

"And this is the trap in which you were caught?"

"It is."

"Will you place your paw in the trap just as you did when you were first caught?"

The bear hesitated, but the man set the trap, and the bear, much against his will, stepped into it.

"Is that how it happened?" asked the fox.

"It is," grumbled the bear, in great pain.

"This, then, is my decree," said the fox solemnly. "Farmer, the bear is at your mercy. He is a born thief. Deal with him as you think best!"

[265]

THE RABBIT'S SELF-RESPECT

One day the rabbit felt very sad. He was thinking what a small creature he was, and how timid he always felt when he met any of the other animals.

"No one in the world is afraid of me," he said to himself in despair, "I must surely be the weakest of all living creatures."

The more he thought of his weakness, the more melancholy he became.

"I may as well make an end of myself," he continued, "for surely I am of no use in the world. No one even respects me. I think I shall jump into this pool of water."

The rabbit stood on the bank of the pool making up his mind to jump, when suddenly an acorn fell from an oak and landed with a splash in the water beside him.

When the rabbit saw this he burst out laughing.

"What a fool I am to think of killing myself!" he shouted. "The acorn is afraid of me! He jumped into the water so that I couldn't catch him!"

The rabbit kept on laughing and went his way happily, for he had found that even he could frighten people and command respect. And this is why he is still alive today.

FINNISH FOLK LORE

The heart of Finnish folk lore is magic. As Lafcadio Hearn has so well said:

"The magic is not like anything else known by that name in European literature. The magic is entirely the magic of words. These ancient people believed in the existence of words, by the utterance of which anything might be accomplished. Instead of buying wood and hiring carpenters, you might build a house by uttering certain magical words. If you had no horse, and wanted to travel rapidly, you would make a horse for yourself out of bits of bark and old sticks by uttering over them certain magical words. But this was not all. Beings of intellect, men and women, whole armies of men, in fact, might be created in a moment by the utterance of these magical words."

These folk tales make much and varied use of the power of words, but they also depict the life of a strange people. Their customs, their beliefs, their sorrows, and their laughter, in short their entire culture, is herein recorded for all time.

The Finns were a pastoral people. They loved their fields and their flocks, their rivers and lakes, and their deep, wild forests. They loved peace, and hated violence. They approved of strength and courage and right doing, and liked nothing better than to trip up the heels of the oppressor and the deceiver. Their ideals were the ideals of true men and women the world over.

On the surface they were cold and inexpressive, and seemed as frozen over as their lakes in winter. But beneath their fur coats their hearts were warm, and deep within their hearts, when least expected, there was a droll laughter, and a keen sense of human values.

For the old and the young alike, these stories are fresh with the dews of the early morning of the world. Older readers will wonder how these ancient people knew so much of the deeper meaning of life, and youth will revel in the brave deeds of adventure and romance, and in the picturesque strangeness of wild nature.

[267]

The authors are indebted to the standard collections of Finnish folk lore: *Suomen kansan satuja ja tarinoita* by Eero Salmelainen and *Suomen kansan satuja* by Iivo Harkonen. They wish, also, to acknowledge their gratitude to Mrs. Margaret Luomajoki Hankila, the dear little grandmother, who has told them stories to which she listened breathless when a wide-eyed little girl sitting at her own grandmother's knee. They have searched to find what is best in the olden treasure-house. They have taken what has seemed best suited to American readers, and what has had in its native language the widest acclaim.

JAMES CLOYD BOWMAN

FINNISH NAMES AND WORDS

The following rules will enable the English reader to pronounce the Finnish words included within the stories:

The Alphabet

The Finnish language is a phonetic language. Every letter of the alphabet is pronounced. No diacritical marks are used. Each letter of the Finnish alphabet is pronounced as herein indicated:

a as in sof*a*	m as in *m*en
ä as in *a*t	n as in *n*et
b as in *b*ed	o as in *o*pen
c as in *c*alm	ö like *er* as in h*er*b
d as in *d*ay	p as in *p*ay
e as in m*e*t	q like *cou* as in *cou*ld
f as in *f*ar	r as in *r*ose
g as in *g*ame	s as in *s*et
h as in *h*ome	t as in *t*ell
i as in d*i*n	u as in p*u*t
j like *y* as in *y*e	v as in *v*est
k as in *k*odak	x as in e*x*press
l as in *l*and	y like the French *u* or the German ü

z like the English z (*z ts* or *s*)

The Vowels

The vowels are a, e, i, o, u, y, ä, ö. The long vowel is indicated by the use of two letters of the same kind as *ii* in L*ii*si or *uu* as in K*uu*man. The short vowel is indicated by the use of a single letter as *i* in *I*mp*i* or *u* and *o* in *U*kk*o*.

[269]

The Diphthongs

The diphthongs which have an exact English equivalent are:

ai as in *a*isle
au like *ow* as in h*ow*
ui as in q*ui*t
oi as in *oi*l
ei as in *ei*ght
ou like *ow* as in l*ow*

Syllables

Words are divided into syllables according to these three common rules:

(a) A single consonant between two vowels must be joined to the following vowel as *m* in Ti-*mo* or *t* in Va-*ti*.

(b) Double consonants are always separated as *kk* in U*k-k*o or *pp* in Ta*p-p*io.

(c) When more than two consonants are found between two vowels, the last consonant is joined to the following vowel as *rtt* in Hu*rt-t*i-nen or *rsk* in my*rs-k*y.

Accent

Finnish words all have the primary accent on the first syllable. If the word is made up of three or more syllables, there is a secondary accent on the third syllable, the fifth syllable, etc.

Vocabulary

Ahnas—avaricious
Äiti—mother
Antti—proper name—boy or man
Arne—proper name—boy or man
Arvo—proper name—boy or man
Aslo—proper name—boy or man

[270]

Helka—proper name—a place
Hellä—gentle
Hiisi—the Evil Power, the same as Lempo
Hiitola—the dominions of Hiisi
Hölmölä—a place name
Hölmöläiset—the people of Hölmölä
Huomenlahja Lipas—hope chest
Hoo—Ho!
Huivi—head shawl
Hurttinen-hosuja—the Dog-Chaser
Hyvästi—good-bye
Iilamanssi—a place name
Ilmarinen—The mighty smith of the Kalevala
Jaakko—Jacob
Joulu—Christmas
Jukka—diminutive for John
Julma—terrible
Ka—look or see
Kala kukko—fish baked in a shell made from rye flour
Kalle—Charles
Kantele—the Finnish harp or zither
Kaunis—pretty
Kiijoki—Kii River
Kipuvuori—Kipu Mountain
Kirjo—book
Kota—a house of bark shaped like a wigwam
Kultani—my dear one
Kyllikki—name of a cow
Kylpy—bath
Kylyn-kylpijä—the Bath-Bather
Leppä—alder
Leski-Akka—widow
Lihan-Syöjä—The Meat-Eater

Liisi—A girl's name
Lippo—dip-net
Louhi—the Mistress of Pohjola
Lounnotar—Daughter of Creation, a name applied to Ilmatar, and other celestial goddesses
Maki—hill
Marja—berry
Martti—Martin
Matti—Matthew
Mielikki—a woman's name
Musti—a cow's name
Niilo—Neil
Noita-Akka—a witch
Oi—Oh
Olavi—Oliver
Olga
Onni—a man's name
Paha-Sydämiset—Sons of the witch, Loviatar
Paholainen—wicked one, imp, devil
Paivankoitto—the dawn
Peikko—imp
Pekka—Peter
Pilkka—mark
Pitkan-Juoksija—the Distance-Runner
Pohjola—the North Country, dark and dismal, sometimes the castle of Louhi
Pölkky—A short thick piece of log
Puuhaara—the fork of a tree
Ruokinen-syöjä—the Food-Eater
Rieska—unleavened bread
Sauna—bath house
Seppo—smith
Sereri—a man's name

Tapio—the God of the Forests
Tauno—a man's name
Timo—a man's name
Toivo—a man's name
Tuonela—the place beyond Tuoni, the River of Death
Tupa—the cottage of the common people
Ukko Untamoinen onnella—the sleeping Old Man of
the Sea
Urho—hero
Uvanto—swamp
Vaino—hostility, malice
Vieno—a woman's name
Vai niin—Is that so?
Vappu—the first day of May
Veden-kantaja—the Water-Carrier
Vendla—a woman's name
Viinan-Juoja—the Wine-Drinker

James Cloyd Bowman (1880–1961) was an English professor at Iowa State University and Northern Michigan University. He published a number of folklore books for children about characters such as Pecos Bill, Winabojo, John Henry, and Mike Fink.

Margery Bianco (1881–1944) was a renowned author of more than twenty-five children's books, including *The Velveteen Rabbit; or, How Toys Become Real.*